"I don't a... anyo...

"I'm the b...

As he wal... ...ita, he looked the picture of c... ...l ease, a long way from the hardworking executive that he was supposed to be, she thought.

"Thus the idle rich," she observed tartly. "I didn't think you were the playboy type."

"I worked hard to get where I am. Do you grudge me a little time off occasionally?"

They wandered past a stream, and Nita couldn't resist a comment on the peacefulness of the scene. "It's so very beautiful."

"Very." But Leon wasn't admiring the scenery; he was looking straight at her. She suddenly felt that familiar jumpy, warming feeling in her body. Could this possibly be caused by Leon?

# Lions
# Walk Alone

## Susanna Firth

# Harlequin Books

TORONTO • NEW YORK • LONDON
AMSTERDAM • PARIS • SYDNEY • HAMBURG
STOCKHOLM • ATHENS • TOKYO • MILAN

Original hardcover edition published in 1983
by Mills & Boon Limited

ISBN 0-373-02564-5

Harlequin Romance first edition August 1983

# CHAPTER ONE

'NITA, he's here again!'

'Who?' Lipstick in her hand, Nita turned away from the brightly-lit make-up mirror to look enquiringly at the girl who had just entered her dressing room.

'That man I was telling you about—you know, the guy who was here last night.'

'Oh, him.' Nita gave another glance at her reflection, frowned critically and then added more blusher to her cheeks with a practised hand. Her mind was more on the performance that she was to give than on news of a total stranger, however great the impression that he seemed to have made on her friend Sandy.

'Is that all you can say? You wouldn't dismiss him as casually as that if you'd seen him,' Sandy rebuked her.

'Probably not. But, as it was my night off and I didn't see him, I'm labouring under a bit of a handicap, aren't I?'

'I *told* you what he was like.'

'So you did.' Not that she had listened very hard. Sandy was always in raptures over some man she had encountered—a different one each day. It was easy to lose track of her extensive love life unless one paid avid attention. 'Tall and dark, didn't you say? That describes about half the men that were on the beach today.'

'None of them could hold a candle to this guy. Believe me, he's absolute dynamite!'

'Love at first sight?' Nita asked wryly, as she slipped out of the towelling robe that she was wearing and reached for the dress that was hanging up against the back of the door.

'Something like that.'

'What about that blond college boy from Michigan? Chuck, wasn't it?'

'He was *last* week, Nita. And anyway, I wasn't serious about him.'

'You're not serious about anyone, that's your trouble.' A faint smile crossed Nita's face. 'You know that. Here, help me with the hooks on this, will you?'

Sandy moved forward to comply, but continued talking as she did so. 'This man could be different. I've got a feeling about him.'

'Oh, yes?' Sandy's infatuations were as shortlived as they were frequent, and Nita had learned to dismiss statements like that with a pinch of salt. 'I wish I had a dollar for every time I've heard you say that—I'd be rich enough to retire by now!'

'Oh, you can laugh.' The other girl tossed back her mane of blonde hair defiantly. 'But you'll be laughing on the other side of your face when he stops by the apartment to take me out.'

'And just how are you going to manage that?'

'I have my methods,' Sandy grinned wickedly. 'He left early last night and I barely had a chance. But tonight——' She paused significantly.

Nita had heard that tone before and it always heralded disaster. 'Sandy, what are you up to?' she demanded.

'If you want something, go find it. That's my philosophy.'

'And you want him?'

'Mm. Who wouldn't?' Sandy looked dreamy. 'He's gorgeous!'

'But how can you? You don't know anything about him. You don't even know his name.'

'I do so know his name. The table was booked for one Leon Calveto.' She rolled the syllables on her tongue, savouring them. 'Leon. That means a lion, doesn't it, Nita?'

'Yes.'

'He looks rather like one. Not in colouring, I mean, his hair's as dark as yours. But there's something about the way that he walks. Like one of the big cats that you see in the zoo. Very sexy.'

'Maybe. But bear in mind that big cats can be dangerous if you don't know how to handle them.'

Sandy laughed. 'I should worry! I've more experience in that line than you, at any rate.'

Nita shrugged. She had to acknowledge the truth of that at least. At nineteen Sandy had packed in more living than most girls her age. And certainly more sexual encounters than herself even though she was three years older. During the five months that they had shared an apartment Nita had watched the other girl's giddy life-style, partly envious, partly disapproving. But whatever the differences between them they were friends nonetheless.

'Don't be a fool! You'll be asking for trouble if you encourage him,' she warned now as she had warned many times before to deaf ears. 'You know the club rules, Sandy. No dates with the——'

'With the clientele. Sure, I know. So what?' Her friend pouted. 'Rules were made to be broken, particularly when they're as dumb as that.. Does the management really expect us to live like nuns?'

'Hardly. But the rules were made for our protection. If you had any sense you'd realise that——'

'I wonder about that, I really do. I think that they're just trying to stop us having a good time.'

'This place has got a good name and they're keen to keep it that way,' persisted Nita. 'If word goes round that any of the girls who work here are easy game, we'll be attracting a very different type of audience before we know it, and that's not what I want. And neither do you, if you think about it.'

Sandy pulled a face. 'Maybe. Do stop lecturing me, Nita!' she added. 'You sound about ninety-nine!'

'I feel it sometimes when you're around,' Nita sighed.

'You needn't worry. I'll be careful. Aren't I always?'

'No.'

'I'm not an idiot, you know.'

'No comment,' Nita laughed.

'Oh, you're impossible! Look, I'm a liberated lady and I can look after myself. O.K.?'

'I suppose so,' Nita admitted reluctantly. 'But it's your funeral.'

'I hope not.' The blonde girl moved towards the door, preparing to leave for her hostess duties at the front of the house. 'I'll take good care. Wish me luck?'

'I'll wish you anything you like, if you'll go away and leave me alone for a while. I'm due on stage in ten minutes and I'm not halfway to ready yet.'

'Better hurry, then. Can't let the management down, can we? And, Nita——'

'Yes?'

'If he's got a brother I'll put in a claim for you, shall I?'

'Out!' Nita picked up a hairbrush and took aim.

With a shriek of laughter Sandy disappeared and the door banged behind her. Nita caught herself smiling. Not that it was a smiling matter at all because Sandy couldn't afford to lose her job. But something about the other girl's lighthearted attitude to life got to her. It was impossible to dislike her for her carefree assumption that the world was placed there for her to enjoy it—a simple way of looking at things, but one that certainly seemed to work for her. Whatever disasters came, she bounced back like a rubber ball. Tears one minute, smiles the next; it was all the same to Sandy.

Automatically Nita made the final adjustments to her hair and make-up and smoothed out the full sleeves of her dress, so that the rows of intricate embroidery with which they were decorated glowed brightly against the creamy-white background. Then, picking up the guitar from the chair beside her, she headed for the stage. She hadn't been called yet, but she liked a little time to herself to absorb the atmosphere and get in the mood of the evening before she went on.

Tonight as she stood in the wings she couldn't get her thoughts away from Sandy. She hoped her friend wasn't serious about this man. He sounded different from her usual type of college boy; older and more experienced, if her description of him was anything like accurate. And with money to spend, if he liked to frequent nightclubs on the level of this one where nothing came cheap. The sort of man who would take his pleasures lightly and then pass on, careless of any broken hearts he might leave behind him.

She heard the sound of applause greeting the dancing act that took the stage before her and gave herself a mental shake. Sandy would have to sink or swim on her own. It was time to concentrate on the job in hand.

'Fabulous audience tonight. You shouldn't have any trouble with them. Not that you ever do.' Bathed in perspiration, his make-up streaked under the heat of the lights, the head of the dancing troupe paused by her side as he came off stage. He was clearly well pleased with his reception. 'Go in and slay them!'

'I'll try,' she promised him.

'Good girl!' With a quick squeeze of her arm he was gone.

'And now for the moment that you've all been waiting for!' Jefferson Peters, the entertainment director, took the stage, microphone in his hand, and flashed a broad grin in Nita's direction before launching into his usual flamboyant introduction of her. 'The star of our show tonight. The Pink Flamingo is proud to present— all the way from the land of gods and fire—Juanita!'

He moved aside, ushering her into the welcoming spotlight, and the applause that greeted her started her adrenalin flowing the way it always did. It was strange how a night's absence sharpened her senses. As she settled herself on the high wooden stool placed ready for her and prepared to launch into her first number Nita could feel a prickle of excitement snake down her spine. She was going to be good tonight. She just knew it.

People had told her before now that she came alive on stage as she did nowhere else. Dazzled by her stage persona, men in particular expected her to generate the same glitter out of the spotlights and were disappointed when it failed to surface. But it was something beyond her control. She just knew that in front of an audience she felt safe and at ease, free to give the best of herself to the work she loved. And tonight was no exception. She felt a surge of happiness as she began to sing.

Normally she was not aware of the different people who made up her audience. They were just an indistinct blur beyond the bright lights that shone on her. Usually she preferred it that way when she performed from the stage. Playing to a warm mass of humanity was simpler than trying to gauge an individual response.

But tonight, as she looked out into the semi-darkness beyond the edge of the stage, smiling and acknowledging the enthusiastic clapping that followed her first number, a man pierced this protective barrier that she put between herself and those who paid to listen to her.

She wasn't sure what it was about him that first drew and held her attention. Certainly he was sitting at one of the front tables, nearest to the stage. But so were a lot of other people. And they were just blank faces to her, whereas this man stood out from the crowd as clearly as if she had been seeking him out.

He was not conventionally good-looking. It was an interesting face, dominated by a strong beak of a nose. He had harsh, rather angular features that were only partially softened by the subdued lighting. A full, sensual mouth and a firm chin that more than hinted at arrogance. Jet-dark hair brushed ruthlessly back from a high, intelligent forehead.

No, not good-looking by any means. But striking. The sort of man to turn female heads when he walked into a room anywhere. Someone who would attract and intrigue women and never lack their company. Yet he seemed to be on his own. Not for long, Nita surmised. He had to be waiting for someone, a wife or a girl-friend. It was too much to suppose that a man like that, in his early thirties or thereabouts, would not have some attendant female.

After she had finished her second song, a catchy Mexican folk tune that set everyone's feet tapping in time to its rhythms, she found her gaze straying in his direction again, curious to see what sort of person had joined him. Probably some super-sophisticated lady, beautifully dressed and coiffeured and made up to the nth degree. A blonde, perhaps; a man as dark as he was might well choose a foil for his own looks. She would be the sort of woman who stood out in a crowd. Not that he would worry about the competition; he could stand it.

But he was still alone, his head turned momentarily away from the stage towards the girl who was serving him with a drink. It was Sandy. With sudden dismay Nita recognised her friend. She was leaning across the table in a deliberately provocative fashion, offering him an excellent glimpse of her full breasts, tantalisingly exposed by her low-cut dress. She was smiling invitingly at him. He could have been the only man in the room; she completely ignored the calls that came from the other guests.

So this was the man that she had been raving about—Leon Calveto. Nita could understand why now. If anything a second glimpse of him had increased Sandy's interest rather than diminishing it. 'Take me, I'm yours.' Everything about her spelled out the message loud and clear to him if he cared to take it up. It was an approach that she had perfected over any number of encounters with male egos and it was one that invariably worked for her.

But Nita could have told her that it wouldn't cut any ice this time. This wasn't a college boy to be dazzled by an obvious show of admiration from an attractive woman. This was a man of the world who would always be the hunter, never the quarry. Why hadn't Sandy the sense to realise that fact? She was a fool to pursue a man like that.

He made his lack of interest all too clear in the way that he tossed some dollar bills on her tray without even bothering to look at her. When she leant forward with an alluring smile to offer him his change he waved her aside with an impatient gesture of his hand that said more clearly than words could have done that he didn't want to know. Nita winced at the expression on Sandy's face, a mixture of hurt pride and disbelief. She wasn't used to being rejected in that offhand manner!

As if he was suddenly conscious of being observed, his head jerked back towards the stage and he was looking directly at Nita before she had a chance to glance away. It was almost as if he could tell that she had been speculating about him. Nita caught her breath as she met his dark eyes and saw the expression in them.

She was used to being stared at, analysed in detail by any number of male glances. It was an occupational hazard and one that she had come to terms with long ago. But there was something different about the way that Leon Calveto looked at her. There was no warmth in his gaze, just critical appraisal. He was studying her like a Roman emperor at a slave auction. And then he raised his glass to her in a mocking salute before he drank from it.

It served her right, she thought, colouring faintly as she looked swiftly down, examining the strings of the guitar that she held for some imagined fault as she strove to regain her composure. She had no business to stare at him like that. But did he have to respond in that manner? As if she had been as obvious as Sandy in expressing her interest in him. Perhaps she had. The thought worried her slightly.

Her backing group played the opening notes of her next song, a sentimental ballad that suited her low, slightly husky voice. As she joined in professionalism took over and she forgot everything but the plaintive melody and the tale of unrequited love that it told. When she finished there was a moment's silence before the applause rang out, a tribute to her artistry. The lights came up again and she got to her feet to bow and smile, a slim figure in a simple white dress.

Nita kept her eyes determinedly away from the corner where the disturbing stranger sat. Even as she settled back on her stool to sing the encore that her audience clearly demanded she ignored the temptation to look, just once, to see if he had received her efforts as enthusiastically as the rest. It didn't matter what he thought of her performance, she told herself. He was nothing to her.

Back in her small dressing room she concentrated on getting ready for her second spot, erasing the unsophisticated girl who had just appeared and replacing her with a woman who knew her way around. A dramatic red dress, cut low across the bust and slashed to show a daring amount of leg at the side, hung ready for her to put on, and Nita eyed it doubtfully. It was the most daring outfit that she had tried yet. Now she was wondering whether it was *too* daring. The memory of Leon Calveto's gaze, stripping her, assessing her, flashed through her mind. What would he make of her now? she wondered.

It was a contrast that usually intrigued her audiences, this transformation from wide-eyed innocence to knowledgeable sophistication, from purity to experience, all in the space of a few minutes. Their reaction never failed to amuse Nita. Stunned surprise was always followed by an even more appreciative reception. The men were particularly enthusiastic, which was hardly surprising. She often thought that it was not the singing they went for, but the selection of barely decent dresses that she wore for the second part of her act.

That was the trouble with this kind of life: it made you cynical. Nita pulled a face at herself in the mirror and concentrated on getting her make-up exactly right, her eyes skilfully outlined, her cheeks and lips ablaze with hectic colour. Then she stepped into the dress and zipped it round her. It clung to every curve of her figure and showed it off superbly. At least she had nothing to be ashamed of.

She was shaking out the folds of chiffon that swirled about her legs when there was a tap at the door. She turned a welcoming smile towards it as she called 'Come in.' Sandy often dropped by about now, taking an illicit few minutes' break from her front of house duties. She would light a cigarette and relax, kicking off her high-heeled shoes and massaging her aching feet as she told funny stories about disasters that had befallen her or one of the other hostesses in the course of the evening.

But it wasn't Sandy tonight. No doubt she was licking her wounds and finding consolation elsewhere, scared that Nita would only say, 'I told you so'. Instead the tow-coloured head and slightly pink features of Jefferson Peters appeared round the door.

'Hi, Jeff. Come on in.'

He pursed his lips in a long, low whistle as he did so. 'That's a stunner, Nita! I haven't seen you in that before, have I? I'd have remembered if I had.'

'I bought it yesterday. And now I'm having doubts.'

'I'm not. You look terrific!'

'Was there something?' Nita cut short the flow. Fulsome compliments annoyed her, however well meant they were.

'I only dropped by to let you know they loved you. But you knew that already, I guess.'

'It's always nice to have it confirmed,' she said lightly.

She sat down before the mirror and waved him casually to a spare chair while she fixed two combs in her hair, Spanish style. They barely kept its dark, springy length in order, but they looked good with this outfit, she knew. Behind her she was aware of Jeff's admiring glance.

'Have dinner with me tonight, Nita?'

'I'll be tired when I finish—you know that. All I really feel like when it's over is flopping into bed.'

He grinned. 'That programme sounds fine by me!'

'A good try, Jeff. But——'

'But not this time. It's O.K.—I get the message.'

Did he? Nita wondered sometimes. They had been dating on and off all season in a fairly casual fashion that allowed each of them to see other people when it suited them. But lately she had begun to get the feeling that it irked Jeff to have made so little headway with her. She hoped that he was not getting different ideas about their future relationship. He was a very pleasant companion when it suited him and also a highly professional colleague. But that was as far as it went, at least on her side.

He was looking a little aggrieved, and she felt faintly guilty. It was the third time that he had asked her out this week and each time she had put him off with some excuse. Perhaps she was being a little unfair.

'Come back to my place for a sandwich and coffee after the show,' she offered impulsively, adding with heavy emphasis, 'And I mean *just* a sandwich and coffee. Don't get any other ideas, will you?' Not that it mattered. Sandy would be there to chaperone them, with a bit of luck.

'I know—you only love your audiences,' he said, resigned to the fact.

'Guessed it in one! Now let me get back to the one I've got waiting for me.' Nita picked up the scarlet flower that stood in a glass of water on her dressing table and pushed it behind her ear.

'Ready?'

'As much as I'll ever be,' she said.

He opened the door for her and she moved eagerly forward.

The songs that she sang in the second half of her act were all about love and passion. They were sultry and seductive, as alluring as the girl who performed them, moving about the audience in a way that sent a beguiling message to every man who looked at her.

It was an approach that Nita had been reluctant to use at first, but Jefferson had talked her into it.

'You're not singing on college campuses any more,' he told her shortly after he signed her up for the season. 'The sort of entertainment that we offer here in Miami Beach is as sophisticated as you'll find anywhere in the States. People expect certain standards or they go some place else. And I need hardly tell you that's the last thing we can afford.'

'I've never done that kind of act before. I wouldn't know where to start,' she argued defensively.

'High time you learnt, then, honey.' And, as she still hesitated, he went on, 'To stay ahead of the game you've got to offer what everybody else does and a little more, otherwise you go under.'

'If you think I'm so behind the times, why did you sign me up in the first place?'

'I saw you had potential and I took a gamble. Don't let me down, Nita.'

'Are you telling me that I lose my job here if I don't go along with your ideas?' she asked directly.

'Hell, no!' His pink face expressed concern. 'You're doing fine. But I'm advising you as a friend. If you want to be successful, be prepared to adapt. That's all I'm saying.'

Nita had the sense to acknowledge the truth of what he said and to be grateful for it in the end. She went to dancing classes and learnt to use her slim, supple body to the best advantage. She let Jefferson talk her into extending her wardrobe to include dresses that she would once have rejected out of hand as too extreme for her—plunge necklines, bare midriffs, skirts cut to show her legs to best advantage. Now she wore them with hardly a qualm. And her repertoire of songs broadened from the simple folk tunes that she had originally confined herself to, including international favourites and old standards.

She was confident that she looked her best tonight as she left the stage to make a slow progress round the room. Jefferson was right when he had said that the audience would like to see her close at hand. The women took the chance to size up her clothes and envy the figure that set them off so well. The men enjoyed the way that she paused in her circuit of the tables, her enormous dark eyes singling out individuals and issuing a tantalising invitation to them.

'*Are you man enough for me?*' she sang, her voice deep and attractive as it sought out every nuance in the words that she was putting over. At this point in the evening she usually stopped to direct lines of her songs at particular males, taking care to select those well-chaperoned by wives or girl-friends. *'Are you man enough to give me what I crave for?'* she went on, and she would invariably raise a shout of laughter as she moved on again with a rueful shake of her head. No one ever took such advances seriously—Nita saw to that!

She was enjoying herself tonight as she steered a skilful path between the tables. She was woman enough to appreciate the warmth in men's eyes as they looked at her, artist enough to approve of the genuine pleasure that her singing was giving. There was a smile on every face.

Except one. Consciously or not, she had started her tour of the floor at the opposite end to that where Leon Calveto sat. She hadn't even looked in his direction as she had continued in a wide semi-circle that took in most of the tables in the room. She didn't know why she had left him until the last. Perhaps she was hoping that he would have gone by the time she reached him. Everyone in the room was riveted to her performance. But that wouldn't stop Leon Calveto from registering a one-man protest if it suited him, she was sure.

But he was still there, his long, well-shaped fingers toying with the glass that held his drink. It looked like Scotch on the rocks. Not for him the fancy cocktails in which the barman specialised, heavy with an assortment of fruit and decorated with a frivolous flamingo in the sugar pink that was the club's colour. A plain man with plain tastes.

And she didn't seem to be one of them. He was looking straight at her, his dark, almost black gaze impersonal, faintly disdainful. Yet there was a challenge there if she cared to read it in the sardonic twist of his mouth. 'Is this the best that you can do?' he was saying to her, more clearly than if he had actually spoken the words. 'Can't you manage anything more polished?'

Nita didn't know what took hold of her. She was just aware of a sudden blaze of anger, rapidly succeeded by a determination to wipe that contemptuous expression off his arrogant face. Just who did he think he was, to walk in here and act as if everyone was less than the dust beneath his feet? First Sandy, now herself. How dared he?

She would make him sit up and notice her, she vowed. And then, when he was well and truly hooked, she would turn away from him, as she had done with all the others. He would know how it felt to be made a fool of in public. And it would serve him right!

'*Are you the man to make me love you?*' She moved closer towards him, singing as she did so, then halted deliberately in front of him, swaying seductively in time to the music. She forced herself to smile enticingly, straight at that hard, ruthless face.

A man would have to be made of stone to resist an appeal like that; Jefferson had told her that often enough. And it had always worked like a charm for her before. At least she had all his attention now. He put down his glass and he was looking at her intently. There was a gleam of something in his eyes. Amusement? Appreciation at the picture she made? Had she cracked him?

'*Are you the man to make me care?*' She sang the next line full at him and extended her arms teasingly towards him. The next move on her part was a quick retreat, a mocking smile as she spun away towards the safety of the stage while the rest of the audience laughed at his discomfiture.

That was the plan. But, even as she moved to carry it

out, he acted. A strong arm snaked out and intercepted her as she turned away, and before she knew what she was about she was gathered up to him, losing her balance as she did so and ending up on his lap.

The audience was indeed laughing, but at Nita's loss of face, not his, as she had intended. As she tried to move away and felt his restraining arm tighten around her, her heart sank. What was it she had said to Sandy? 'Big cats can be dangerous if you don't know how to handle them'. What on earth had made her provoke this one to the point of retaliation?

The steel band around her forced her close, uncomfortably close, to him. Pressed against the strong wall of his chest, she could feel the steady beat of his heart against her. It took no effort at all on his part to restrain her attempts to free herself. He wasn't even breathing any faster and the sardonic expression on his face had, if anything, deepened.

'Let me go!' she muttered furiously at him.

'When I'm ready.' His voice was deep and as attractive as Sandy had claimed, she thought irrelevantly. It was tinged with the faintest trace of a foreign accent. He raised it slightly now, mocking her attempts to get away from him. 'Don't leave me, sweetheart. Take pity on a man who wants to take up the invitation you're offering to him.'

The microphone in her hand picked up that statement as he intended that it should and the audience received it rapturously. Some even clapped their encouragement. A quick glance round her revealed that even the members of her backing group had collapsed in laughter at her plight.

Leon Calveto was smiling now. He might well. He had certainly turned the tables on her with a vengeance!

'This isn't a joke,' she told him in an undertone that she hoped would not reach general circulation, forcing a smile on to her face to show the onlookers that she was taking everything well.

'Isn't it? We must have a different sense of humour.' There was mockery in the dark eyes that flicked over her, registering the fury that seethed within her.

'All right, so you've had your little bit of fun at my expense. But it's over now.'

'Is it?' He flung back his head and laughed in genuine amusement. 'I don't think so, somehow. I've got a notion it's just beginning.'

'Then you're wrong.'

'I don't think so,' he said.

'I never want to lay eyes on you again! Do you understand that?'

'Perfectly,' he said, unmoved. 'But never is a long time.'

'In my opinion it's not nearly long enough!'

A dark brow lifted in faint amusement. 'Then I'd better give you something to remember me by, hadn't I?'

Nita guessed what his next action was going to be, but she was given no chance to take evasive measures. He had the situation too much under control for that. His hand slipped upwards to press against the bare skin of her back and she stiffened in reaction.

'No!' she protested, although she knew he would not listen.

'Don't scream,' he said as he pulled her closer to him. 'They might think you're enjoying yourself, and that would never do, would it?'

'You——'

Her reply was lost as his mouth descended on hers, plundering her lips with an insistence that shocked her.

She had kissed before, of course—she wasn't a complete stranger to physical contact with a man. But she had never suffered a forced intimacy like this, and certainly not in front of a couple of hundred interested observers.

He could force himself on her because he had outmanoeuvred her, she told herself. But he couldn't force a response from her. She wouldn't fight him. That would be undignified and humiliating. But she would lie there in his arms like a dead weight until he chose to release her. Let him see what satisfaction that gave him! No man took that sort of treatment for very long.

But her body betrayed her, ignoring the messages that she gave it. Whispers of sensation thrilled down her spine as his fingers stroked her skin, before moving to the nape of her neck and caressing it with feather-light strokes. Try as she would, she could not resist the hard, sensual demands of his mouth. Her lips parted to admit him, allowing him to stir her to a response.

And then she was lost and she knew it. Waves of pleasure ran riot through her body, making her aware of nothing but the man whose body pressed so close to hers. The tang of the spicy cologne he wore drifted to her nostrils, adding further to her sensual appreciation of him. He roused her fully, stirred her as no man had ever managed to do before now. She no longer entertained any thoughts of fighting him. Her body spoke all too clearly of his complete conquest of her.

The lights, the room, even the sound of the amused audience that was witnessing the embrace, they all faded away to nothingness as she closed her eyes and let sensation take over. Her arms crept round him, holding him closer to her. She was oblivious to everything except the man who was creating this ecstasy.

But Leon Calveto had other ideas, Nita soon

discovered. He wrenched himself away from her, pushing her roughly aside. He was in no danger of losing control, she realised bitterly. The shock came like a bucket of cold water in her face, instantly sobering her. It took no effort at all for him to call matters to a halt. Either he had superhuman restraint or he simply didn't give a damn for what she had to offer him.

It was the latter, of course. He had never forgotten that they had an audience, even if she had. It had all been an exhibition for the onlookers, a public demonstration of the power that he had over women. And, if it put her in her place for challenging that authority in the first instance, all to the better.

In that moment of realisation Nita hated him.

'You swine!' she breathed furiously.

Leon Calveto gave her a mocking glance. 'Sorry I stopped?' Without waiting for an answer he turned away from her and, picking up the microphone which she had left carelessly dangling on its lead, he announced to the room at large, 'The show's over, ladies and gentlemen. I hope you enjoyed watching as much as I did taking part!'

There was laughter and sporadic applause. Nita felt her cheeks burning with a combination of rage and humiliation. She supposed she couldn't slap his arrogant face here, although her fingers itched to do so.

He read her intentions loud and clear. 'I shouldn't if you value your job here,' he warned her. 'The customer is usually right in this part of the world.'

'You swine! Will you let me go?'

'A lady would have said please.' But he released her.

'But I'm no lady, am I? You've made that abundantly clear.'

'I'm glad you got the message.'

And, as Nita turned without a word and headed for the safety of backstage, she shivered at the cold contempt in his tone.

## CHAPTER TWO

NITA was shaking like a leaf with reaction when she reached her dressing room. Too shattered even to make her way to a chair and sit down, she leant for a long moment against the door, fighting a battle to control herself.

It was a long time since anyone had managed to get beneath the cool, detached mask that she presented to the world. It was an act that she had trained herself to put on in the last few years and that she thought was well nigh impossible to see through.

Leon Calveto had shown her the foolishness of imagining she was immune. He had stripped aside that surface veneer as easily as if it had never existed and had exposed the mass of vulnerable nerve ends that still seethed underneath. Nita told herself that no man would ever succeed in getting to her again. No man was going to hurt and humiliate her as one man had done in the past.

Yet Leon Calveto had done both in the space of a very brief encounter. Nita stared at herself, reflected in the long mirror on the other side of the room. Was this flushed, tumbled girl really the cool, professional artiste who was always calm and who boasted that nothing threw her?

She had lost one of her combs and her hair rioted in dark disorder over her face, the scarlet flower that she tucked carefully behind one ear now sticking out at a rakish angle. Her eyes were bright with suppressed emotion, her cheeks flushed with a colour that owed little to artifice now. And her lips were the biggest giveaway of all, bruised and swollen with passion.

She looked cheap and she felt it. Anger fought with humiliation and won after a short struggle. Damn Leon Calveto! She wasn't going to collapse in a heap and cry her heart out. She wouldn't give him that satisfaction, whether he knew about it or not.

She moved forward and stripped off the red dress, tossing it carelessly into an untidy heap on the floor. However much it had cost her to buy, she wasn't sure that she would be wearing it again. It would hold too many bad memories for her. The scanty underclothes that she had worn beneath it followed quickly, and then she stepped into the shower cubicle that was one of the perks of having the star dressing room. It meant that she had little space besides to spread herself and her possessions, but Nita didn't mind that. After three years of sharing washing and dressing facilities a place to herself was heaven.

The cool, stinging needles of water braced and revived her and she began to relax slightly as she stood there, soaping herself vigorously, as if by that means she could erase the memory of those long, lean fingers moving across her skin in practised caresses. If she scrubbed hard enough perhaps she could even cancel out the knowledge of her own response to them.

She refused to allow herself to wonder why *that* man of all men had the power to send waves of sensation rocketing through her body. She didn't want to know, she told herself firmly. She didn't care. It was an isolated incident that would not be repeated. After tonight Leon Calveto would move on. And, after tonight, she would forget his existence.

There was a tap at the door and she roused herself reluctantly. That would be Jeff, coming to collect her so that they could go on to her place for the coffee and sandwiches that she had offered him. He was quick tonight. Usually, when they had a date after the show, it was she who ended up waiting for him. He was conscientious about his work and liked to make sure that everything was in order backstage before he went off duty. Quite often he was delayed with talk about future plans and projects, post-mortems on things that had gone wrong in the night's show or arguments about lighting or staging.

She didn't feel like seeing him now. If truth were told, she didn't feel like seeing anyone. But that wasn't his fault.

'Come in,' she shouted through the noise of hissing water. 'I'm just in the shower. Hang around for a bit, will you? I won't be long.'

She heard a grunt of assent and saw his figure hazily through the frosted glass as he entered and took a seat to wait for her. Reluctantly she began to rinse herself.

'Did you hear what that madman did to me?' she called. If he hadn't seen it himself, someone was bound to have told him. It was too good a story not to circulate the length of the club and beyond. Nita could imagine the good-natured teasing that she would have to endure over the next few days. 'A fine lot of Sir Galahads we have on the staff here! No one lifted a finger to help me. And that bunch of layabouts that you grace with the name of musicians were as useless as the rest. They just split their sides laughing at me.'

Another grunt reached her as Jeff's only response.

'I'll tell you something,' she said loudly. 'If I ever see that guy again, I'll give him a piece of my mind! I should have hit him where it hurts. I wish I had now, it would have served him right. The conceit of that man!'

'Mm.' Perhaps Jeff didn't want to waste time discussing it here and now. He sounded a little impatient. He would be ready to eat, Nita guessed. She reached for her towel, rubbing herself down briskly.

'Sorry to keep you. Sling me my robe, will you?' she asked him. 'It's over by the door.'

She heard him step across the room and return, and expected the towelling wrap to appear over the top of the cubicle. Instead the door opened and male figure loomed into view.

She held a scanty towel against her breasts. 'Jeff, do you mind? This isn't a private peepshow.'

'Isn't it? It sounded like an invitation to one, from what you were just saying.'

A pair of mocking dark eyes that most certainly did not belong to Jeff scanned her figure with lazy ease.

'What the hell are you doing here?' she demanded.

'You didn't think I was finished with you, did you? I wanted to see a little more of you.' Leon Calveto's deep tones managed to make the words insulting.

'How dare you!' She snatched her robe from his grasp and manoeuvred her way into it, hoping she wasn't providing him with too much of a glimpse of naked flesh as she did so. Then she pushed past him into the room, brushing against him as she did so and recoiling at the contact as if he had been red-hot.

'It's all right, I don't have the plague,' he told her, noting the gesture as she had known that he would.

'No?' she asked tartly. 'Pardon me if I disagree.'

In a room the size of a pocket handkerchief it was almost impossible to distance oneself from anybody, friend or foe, but she did the best she could, stationing herself discreetly near the house telephone. She thought she could handle this herself, but it was good to know that assistance was at hand if she cared to summon it.

'How did you get in here anyway?' she asked.

'It wasn't difficult.' He took a spare chair and sat down as if the visit was going to be a prolonged one.

'I shouldn't make yourself too comfortable—you're not stopping.'

'No?' A dark brow rose in what she thought was faint amusement. Damn the man! Why couldn't he treat her like a rational human being?

'Patrons aren't allowed backstage.' She didn't say she was sorry.

'So the sign said. But I didn't choose to observe it.'

'And what did you do with the house detective who sits alongside it? Did you ignore him too?' Boris was two hundred and eighty pounds and an ex-wrestler. As obstacles went he wasn't easily circumvented.

'I told him my name was Leon Calveto and that I was a friend of yours.'

'And he believed you.'

He shrugged. 'Why not? And a fifty-dollar bill is a fair inducement for a man to turn a blind eye, wouldn't you say?'

'I'm sorry you had to waste so much money,' she said coldly.

'I wouldn't call it a waste,' he said carelessly. 'I'd calculate that I've had about a dollar's worth of my entrance fee so far and I expect to see a return on the rest before the night is through.'

Any notion that Nita had that he had come here to

apologise for his earlier behaviour faded rapidly. So what did he want with her? Anger flamed within her, just below the surface, ready to take hold and banish the initial fear that she had of him.

'If you've come here to be deliberately unpleasant——' she began.

'I haven't.'

'It sounds suspiciously like it to me,' she flared. 'So what *do* you want with me?'

'I came to ask you to have dinner with me,' he said imperturbably.

'Dinner and what else?' So that was his game, was it? Some men were so thick-skinned! Did Leon Calveto really think she fancied him in spite of all the things that he had just heard her say about him? She laughed, a hard sound, devoid of humour. 'No.'

'That's not a word I'm accustomed to hearing.'

She shrugged in her turn. 'Too bad.'

He studied her through narrowed eyes. 'Talking of being deliberately unpleasant, I've had more gracious replies when I've asked a lady out to dinner.'

'On your own admission I'm no lady!' she snapped.

'All right then. If that's how you feel about it, I'll use the other approach.' He leaned back in his chair and said calmly, 'What's it worth to you?'

She made an incredulous sound. 'Do you mean money?'

'Interested you, have I?' He voiced his contempt. 'Yes. I mean money. How much?'

'You couldn't pay my price.'

'Try me and see,' he drawled.

'If you think you can buy me the way that you bought Boris, you've got another think coming, Mr Calveto. Besides,' she smiled sweetly at him, 'I already have a date.'

'Break it,' he commanded her imperiously.

'I don't choose to.'

'Can he offer you what I can offer you, do you think?'

'If you mean money, probably not,' she said steadily. 'And before you start parading a list of your other good points, I'll concede that he's not as striking to look at as you are either. But he is kind, considerate, polite and a whole lot of other things that you'll never be if you try for a thousand years. Do I make myself clear?'

'As crystal.' But he still made no move to go, as insolently at his ease as ever, his long legs stretched out before him, his hands buried in the pockets of his immaculately cut trousers. 'How about breakfast tomorrow?'

'No.'

'I see. He usually stays on for breakfast, does he, this paragon of all virtues?'

Nita's first instinct was to deny the charge hotly, her second to let it pass unchallenged. If he thought she was that committed to another man he would lose interest perhaps.

'And, if he does, it's no business of yours as far as I can see.' Her head tilted defiantly at him.

'None at all.' He gave a thin smile. 'Lunch, then?'

'You really can't take no for an answer, can you? I didn't believe you when you said that before.'

'I'm used to getting what I want.'

'And that includes another man's leavings?' she taunted him. 'I wouldn't have thought you were the type.'

'A compliment at last?'

'Make the most of it. There won't be any more,' she said shortly. 'Charming though this little interlude has been, I think it's time to bring it to a halt. I want to get dressed.'

'Don't let me stop you. But, if he's got any red blood about him, I'm sure he'll prefer you the way you are now.' His eyes rested on the golden expanse of skin revealed by her skimpy robe.

Nita resisted the urge to adjust the garment more securely round her. It would only amuse him. 'Are you going?' she asked him.

'Not yet.'

'I'll have you thrown out,' she threatened. Her hand went to the phone and lifted the receiver.

'Leave that.' His hand came out and covered hers. Its hard strength half thrilled, half scared her. 'You'd regret it afterwards.'

'I can't think why.'

For a moment Nita defied him, her fingers resisting the lean tension of his. She hadn't really any option, she knew. If he chose to, he could make her listen to him. Nita gave in before it came to that. Pointedly she removed her hand from his, as if his touch defiled her, and made a show of consulting the dainty watch that adorned her wrist. 'I'll give you three minutes. Make the most of them.'

'I came here because I wanted to talk to you——'

'*Just* to talk to me?' she interrupted him with heavy sarcasm. 'Of course, I should have known from the start that you were a gentleman, shouldn't I? You didn't want to lay a finger on me.'

'Who's being conceited now?' he drawled. 'There are men around who can resist your undoubted attractions, you know.'

'Sure. But your behaviour this evening didn't give me much indication that you were one of them,' she told him.

'Just testing,' he said. 'Besides, I wanted to establish contact.'

'You did that all right!'

'Aren't you going to ask me why?'

'If it wasn't for the usual reasons that a man is interested in a woman I really couldn't say. But I'm sure you're about to enlighten me.'

'I'm a fellow countryman of yours.'

Nita had already identified that tinge of accent. She could have conducted this whole conversation in Spanish if she had chosen to. But she had her own reasons for not doing so. It was three years since she had used that language for anything except her stage work. She had no intention of using it now.

'No, Mr Calveto,' she said coldly, 'not a fellow countryman. I'm sorry if you've been misled by my publicity, but I'm an American citizen. So now that we've discovered yet one more thing that we don't have in common, are you going to leave me in peace, or do I have to call for help?'

He ignored the question and went on smoothly, 'You can hold an American passport because you were born here. And your mother was American—from Virginia, to be precise. Your father was working over here in Miami when he met her. Strange how history repeats itself, isn't it?'

Nita said nothing.

He continued, his dark eyes on her face, studying it relentlessly for a trace of a reaction to what he was telling her. 'You lived here until you were five years old. And then your father did what he always intended to do when he'd accumulated enough money and experience at his job. He went back home to Mexico and took his wife and child with him.'

'All very interesting,' she said tonelessly. Her face had paled and one hand drummed nervously against the top of the dressing table.

'Isn't it? And I can go on, if you'd like me to——'

'No,' she said abruptly. 'I don't want to hear any more.'

'A pity, because I know all the details. Every one.'

'I'm sure you're very well informed,' Nita said scornfully.

'Aren't you going to ask me how I know all this?' he prompted her softly.

He was playing with her like a cat with a helpless mouse. He could have told her all this at the beginning. Instead he had chosen otherwise. She shivered, panic suddenly striking her. She had no doubt at all that Leon Calveto was speaking the truth. He had already said enough to convince her. She had never talked to anyone about her background—there had been no point; it no longer concerned her. That part of her life lay behind a closed door.

'I——' She started to speak and halted abruptly. She didn't know what to say to him.

'Nita, love, are you ready? I'll eat six plates of those sandwiches you promised me and then have you for dessert. How does that——'

Jeff's cheerful face appearing round the door made a sudden break in the tension that was building up in the room.

'Oh!' He took in her visitor, sitting there as if he owned the establishment. 'Pardon me, I didn't know you had someone with you.'

'Jefferson Peters, Leon Calveto.' Nita made the introductions reluctantly, then saw frowning recognition dawn on Jeff's face as he looked closer. She had no need to wonder whether he had witnessed the fiasco that had been her second spot this evening. Clearly he had. His acknowledgement of the other man was curt to the point of rudeness.

'Jefferson is our entertainment director,' she explained. She hoped there wasn't going to be trouble. The last thing she wanted was for the two of them to be fighting over her like dogs squaring up over a juicy bone.

But Leon Calveto seemed inclined to be gracious. 'Indeed? Then let me congratulate you on an excellent show here tonight.'

'I'm glad you enjoyed it.' Jeff still looked belligerent.

'Some parts more than others, I must confess.' The other man's sardonic glance rested for an instant too long on Nita, his meaning abundantly clear.

Jeff met provocation with provocation. 'Nita's got a great act going. I'm lucky to have her. And she has some pretty dynamic off-stage talents too, haven't you honey?'

Nita frowned at him. She didn't like the way that they were both scoring points off each other at the expense of her reputation. 'That's enough, Jeff!' She didn't dare say that to Leon Calveto.

'And modest with it. She's got it all!'

'I'm sure she has.' But it was scepticism, not agreement, that Nita heard in the Mexican's reply.

'That's my girl,' said Jeff. Was it by accident or design that he stressed the personal pronoun?

There was an awkward pause. Awkward for Nita at least. Jeff was clearly waiting for his opponent's next move, expecting it to be retreat. And that opponent was equally clearly standing his ground.

Nita didn't know what she wanted. She would like nothing better than to see the door close after that tall, striking figure with the knowledge that she need never lay eyes on him again. But she couldn't afford to let him go, not without knowing what brought him here and exactly what was behind the remarks that he had made to her before Jeff's untimely interruption.

And he knew it, damn him. She could tell from the mocking lift to his mouth as he watched her. The female mind didn't present any mysteries for Leon Calveto. He could tell exactly what sort of reaction he had stirred up in her and he was relishing every moment of her discomfort.

Jeff wasn't going to like this. Men never did like losing face. But she would smooth things over with him as soon as she had the chance, Nita thought optimistically.

'Mr Calveto—that is—Leon has asked me to have dinner with him tonight.'

'Has he? I thought I was the lucky guy.'

'We could make it some other time?' Her tone was appealing. 'Leon's not in town for very long and he's an old friend,' she lied glibly, surprising herself.

'An old *friend*, huh?' Jeff gave a harsh laugh of disbelief. After all, he had seen that very public embrace. For a long moment she thought that he was going to make an issue out of it. Then, perhaps realising that he would look a fool if he did, he gave in with a careless, 'O.K., honey, if that's the way you want it. As you say, there'll always be another time. That's how you like it, isn't it?' He turned to go with a nod at the other man. 'Variety's the spice of life where our Nita's concerned. But, as you're an old friend, I guess you'd know that already.'

He didn't wait for a reply and the door banged behind him. Then the sound of cheerful whistling and he was gone.

He might well whistle, thought Nita furiously. He had just got his own back on her in the neatest way possible. Who said men weren't as bitchy as women if they chose to be? If she had been hoping for any kind of romantic evening with Leon Calveto that comment of Jeff's would have been guaranteed to kill it stone dead.

The way things stood, of course, it didn't really matter what he thought of her morals; they didn't concern him. But she didn't like anybody to get the wrong impression, and she turned to explain.

'Jeff is——'

'Of no interest at all to me, whatever place you claim that he does or does not occupy in your life,' he said in a bored tone. 'Now, the sooner you dress yourself, the sooner we can go and find something to eat.'

'I'm not hungry,' she said childishly.

'I am. Anyway, we have things to discuss and I've wasted enough time already.'

Her time was of no account, of course! Nita seethed. But she reached for her clothes nonetheless. She wanted nothing so much as to defy him, but she couldn't. Not if she wanted to find out more. And, however much she might deny it, she did want to hear more. And they both knew it.

She assumed that Leon would offer to leave the room while she dressed. But he made no move to do so and she was forced to ask him to wait outside for her.

'I've already seen all you have to offer,' he drawled, his tone making it insultingly clear that it held no charms at all for him. 'Don't tell me maidenly modesty still operates in your case.'

'Not at all,' she snapped. 'Just choosiness. When I give a private show I like to perform before an invited audience. Any objections?'

'None at all.' He got to his feet, his tall figure
immediately dominating the room. 'It's a pleasure that I
can forgo without too many regrets.'

He couldn't have made it more obvious that her kind of
woman didn't do anything for him, Nita thought, as the
door closed behind him and she began to dress herself
automatically. He despised her for what he considered her
to be—someone with no morals to speak of.

And yet he had business with her—or so he claimed.
She frowned as she stepped into her simple cotton skirt
and pulled a matching pink T-shirt over her head and
tucked it in the waistband. What did he want? Fears
and doubts rose in her mind.

It wasn't long before she joined him outside the
dressing room, although he didn't waste words
complimenting her on the fact. His women probably
never dared to keep him waiting.

But Nita wasn't one of his women, as his hard,
unsmiling face and brusque manner made eminently
clear.

'Ready?'

'Yes.' As much as she ever would be when it came to
dealing with him, she supposed.

'I've a table booked at the Primavera.' He named a
small Italian restaurant that she had often visited with
Jeff. It wasn't far away from the club.

'I know it.'

'Do you mind walking there? I can get a cab if you
would prefer?'

'No, don't bother.' Nita didn't know that she wanted
to sit beside him in the enclosed space of a car. And
anyway, on this section of the Beach, well patrolled and
policed even at this time of night, it was safe enough to
go on foot without worry.

Leon Calveto didn't attempt to take her arm as she thought he might, but she was conscious enough of his powerful figure, silent at her side, and held herself tensely, careful to keep a distance between them.

She was relieved when they reached the restaurant and the width of a stout wooden table separated them. They were seated slightly apart from the main dining area, in an alcove that was intended for cosy tête-à-têtes. If only the waiter who was smiling so benignly at them knew how far from being an ideal couple they were!

'A drink?' Leon slanted an enquiring look in her direction.

'Why not?' Nita ordered a vodka on the rocks and saw the faint lift to his brow. 'You're thinking that nicely brought up girls from our part of the world don't order drinks like that.'

'Perhaps.' He ordered a Scotch for himself and then turned back to her. 'But you've put all that behind you, haven't you?'

'I hope so.' And she thought she had succeeded until tonight when this man had appeared on the scene. 'The past is just that. It doesn't have any meaning for me any more.'

'I see.' He paused as their drinks were served. 'And what about the people in your past?'

She reached for her glass and took a steadying sip of the ice-cold liquid within. It wasn't often that she indulged in spirits, but tonight she had felt in need of Dutch courage. It looked as if her instincts were right.

'What about them?' she responded warily.

'You care nothing about them either, I suppose?' he asked her.

'Should I? I have a new life now. I wouldn't have anything in common with the girls I grew up with.'

'Or they with you, I imagine.' The brown eyes scanned her with faint contempt. 'But I wasn't referring to them.'

'No?' She took another drink and pretended an interest in the menu she held. She knew where he was heading now. She had known all along, but she had refused to admit it to herself, let alone him.

'No. You're not obtuse, so don't pretend that you've no idea what I'm talking about.' He frowned, his dark brows drawing together in a hostile line. 'I mean your father.'

'I haven't a father,' she said. 'Not any more.'

He made an impatient noise.

'It's true. If you know as much about me as you claim, you should know that,' Nita told him bitterly.

'I know it's suited you to ignore his existence for these last three years.'

'Is that what he told you?'

'It's what I've heard from other people.'

'And you believed them, of course.' Nita's glass hit the table with an angry thump.

He didn't reply. At that moment a waiter appeared to remind them that they hadn't ordered yet.

'What will you have?' Leon's tone was as abrupt as hers had been, impatient at the interruption.

The lines of print danced off the menu page at her. Food was the last thing on her mind at the moment. 'Oh, anything.' She made a random choice. 'The snapper, I think, with a side salad. No, nothing else.'

He made his own selection and ordered a bottle of wine without consulting her preferences. She wondered if this conversation was as much of a strain for him as it was for her. If it was he gave no indication of it.

'What do you want with me?' she asked bluntly. 'Who exactly are you anyway?'

'You know my name.'

Who was being deliberately obtuse now? 'You know what I mean!'

'Call me an interested party,' he said.

'Interested in what?'

'Taking you back home.'

'My home is here in Florida now,' she said coldly.

'Even if your father thinks otherwise?'

'My father doesn't control my actions any more,' Nita said calmly. 'I thought that he would have realised that by now.'

'Perhaps he has. But he wants you back.'

'Does he?' She gave him a direct look. 'Is that what you've come to tell me? Three years ago he said he never wanted to see me again.'

'And you believed him?'

'He usually means what he says—that's how he got where he is. Straight talking, no frills, just the truth, whether it's pleasant or not.' Nita closed her eyes to hide the hurt that must surely show in them. She hadn't thought that her father's business rules would apply in her case. But they had. Leon Calveto couldn't know what she had been through when her letters had come back unopened and her attempts to get in touch had been rejected out of hand. 'Don't tell me he's changed his mind?'

'He needs you.'

'Did he say so?' Nita demanded.

'Not in so many words.'

'What *did* he say?'

He shrugged. 'That, if I found you, I could tell you that you were free to come home, if you cared to.'

'Yes, that sounds like him,' Nita said wryly. 'Graciousness was never one of his strong points. It's not exactly the fatted calf, is it?'

'Do you think that you deserve that from him?'

'I've never expected it, at any rate.' She wasn't going into the rights and wrongs of the matter with a total stranger. 'Where do you come into all this anyway?' she demanded of him. 'Is it money you're after? Do you get a handsome pay-out once the erring daughter has been restored to the fold?'

His face darkened with anger and she knew she had touched him. 'Money! Is that the first thing that comes to mind with you?' he asked contemptuously.

'It's a consideration.'

'Not where I'm concerned.'

He certainly looked prosperous enough. The suit he was wearing was hand-tailored and the heavy watch on his wrist had looked expensive. But looks weren't everything in a man. She had learnt that lesson by now.

'So?' she asked. 'Enlighten me.'

There was a flurry of activity at their side as their meal arrived and Leon was silent as it was served, approving the wine before it was poured into their glasses. When they were left alone again, he deigned to explain matters to her.

'I'm a business associate of your father. I've known him for some time. We've always got on well.' A genuine smile lit the harsh planes of his face and gave him a human look for the first time. Nita was amazed at the difference it made to him. 'He chose to confide in me about his personal life——'

'And you volunteered to solve his problems for him. That was very obliging of you,' she said sarcastically. 'Tell me, was my father grateful to you?'

'He said I was a damn fool for interfering.'

She laughed shortly. 'Then why did you?'

'I thought it was time that things were patched up

between you.' The dark eyes flicked over her. 'You're all he's got.'

'However unsatisfactory.' Nita was quick to voice his unspoken comment. She picked moodily at the food on her plate, not really tasting what she ate as she tried desperately to take in what she had been told. Three years out in the cold and now the olive branch—or something fairly close to it. She knew her father. However ungracious the message, it meant just that.

'So why the change of heart?' she asked.

'Does there have to be a reason?'

'My father usually has a reason for everything he does. I can't imagine him making an exception in this case.'

'Time softens people.'

'Nothing short of a major earthquake would have that effect on him,' she said derisively. Then she saw his face, the jerk of a small muscle by that hard, unyielding mouth. 'Something's happened, hasn't it?'

'Would you care if it had?'

'My father? How is he? Is he all right?'

'I wondered when you were going to get round to asking that,' Leon said grimly.

'Well? Tell me.'

He didn't try to soften the news or lead up to it gradually. 'He had a heart attack a little over two weeks ago.'

Nita gripped the table edge hard in an effort to control herself. Suddenly the room was spinning around her. 'Bad?'

'Bad enough,' he told her unemotionally. 'Stress, the doctors said—that and overwork.'

'He always did work too hard.' As long as she could remember, work had been her father's life. Her mother and herself had seemed to come a long way behind it in his affections. 'He didn't send for me.' That hurt her.

'How could he? He didn't know where you were,' Leon Calveto pointed out with cruel emphasis. 'You didn't see fit to furnish him with your address, so I had to get an agency in to track you down.'

She hardly heard him. The news had stunned her. Diego Lopez had always seemed invincible, an iron man with an iron will that had shown itself as much to his only child as to his business rivals. Illness had never touched him in his life. Until now, it seemed.

'How is he now?' Nita asked.

'Recovering.'

'You don't give much away, do you?' she flared.

He shrugged. 'I'm not his doctor.'

'I must go to him,' she said.

'A bit late in the day for daughterly devotion. But better late than never, I suppose.'

'I love my father!' Nita claimed furiously.

'Do you? You don't seem to have shown much proof of it in the last three years.'

'How dare you speak to me like that!'

'I speak as I find,' he shrugged.

'You'll find you're wrong.'

'I hope so,' he said.

But his tone lacked conviction.

## CHAPTER THREE

NEXT day, as she sat in the cool, air-conditioned comfort of a plane bound for Mexico City, Nita's head was still spinning from the speed at which events had overtaken her. It all seemed a bit like a dream—or rather a nightmare, orchestrated by the man who now occupied the seat beside her.

'Comfortable?' Leon Calveto's dark head turned towards her in polite enquiry.

'Fine, thank you.'

Communications between them were on a civilised basis today, as if last night's encounter had never taken place. But Nita had not forgotten it, and she was sure that he hadn't either.

She looked warily sideways at him. He was every inch a businessman, smart in a sombre suit teamed with a cream silk shirt and a discreetly patterned tie. But the outward trappings couldn't conceal the true nature of the man, the particular, predatory appeal that he had for women. Nita had seen the interest flare in the stewardess's eyes as she had seated them. 'I'm Susie. Call me if you need anything at all,' she had said to them both, but her invitation was directed solely at Leon.

She was welcome to him, if she wanted him. Any woman could have him as far as Nita was concerned. Yes, he had sexual magnetism. But that was all he had to offer. His other qualities were less appealing to live with—his arrogance, his automatic assumption that he

45

knew best, his tendency to judge without hearing the facts. They added up to a rude, overbearing boor, Nita told herself.

She smiled her acceptance of a spare pillow and a pile of the latest glossy magazines to read on the journey and sipped the glass of champagne that one of the stewards offered her. It was three years since she had enjoyed the privileges that made for a first-class lifestyle, but it was amazing how quickly one settled back into a world where other people took care of the details of one's life, smoothing out the minor irritations that occurred. The very rich led a cocooned existence.

Careful, she warned herself. Don't get used to all this luxury. This isn't happy-ever-after land that you're heading for. You discovered that a long time ago. She gave a little sigh.

That attracted Leon's attention. He didn't miss a thing.

'What's the matter?' he asked.

'Nothing.'

A dark brow lifted sardonically. 'It doesn't look like it.' He glanced across her to the window and the view it gave of the rapidly receding Florida coastline. 'Well, it's too late to change your mind now.'

'I'm quite aware of that, thank you,' she said coldly. 'And anyway, I haven't changed my mind.'

'Then stop sulking and make the best of it.'

'I'm trying to.'

'Really?' He was sceptical. 'I can't say that I've noticed much evidence of it.'

So much for her attempts to be politely distant to him. Trust him to misinterpret them!

'Surely you'll allow me a few regrets?' she asked coldly.

'For what you've left behind?' He sounded disbelieving. 'And what exactly does that amount to?'

'Quite a lot—at least by my standards. My career for a start. And then there are my friends——'

'Your career!' He was rudely, bitingly dismissive. 'Ah, yes—top of the bill in a squalid little nightclub. Was that the summit of your ambition? Should I apologise for dragging you away from stardom? I'm not going to.'

'Squalid, it isn't!' Nita sprang to her own defence. 'The Pink Flamingo has got a very good reputation.'

'For what, I wonder?'

'For entertaining people,' she snapped.

'Oh, that I don't doubt. But as to the kind of entertainment offered——' His mouth twisted contemptuously.

'Substandard?' Nita asked sweetly. 'You think I can't sing?'

'You sing very nicely.' He managed to make it sound like a put-down.

'Thank you. You're very kind,' she said rudely.

'But it was your other assets that I was referring to.'

'Oh?' She feigned ignorance. 'And what are they?'

'Do you really need me to list them?' His dark eyes flicked over her figure, making a swift but obvious inventory. 'I'd have thought you knew precisely what you had to offer, from the way that you were flaunting yourself at every man in sight last night.'

Not every man, she thought. Just you. She had hardly been able to drag her eyes away from him, for all she knew that he spelled danger. And it was the first time she had felt such a wave of sexual awareness and excitement in an encounter. But it was no use expecting Leon Calveto to believe that. She wasn't even sure that she wanted him to. After all, she had her pride.

She forced herself to give a careless laugh. It took an effort to sound casual when she was burning inside with the resentment that his words caused. 'The club likes us to make the customers feel welcome,' she defended.

'I don't doubt it.'

'And you're saying that's a bad thing? I don't think that anyone else who was there last night would agree with you.'

'Probably not. But other people's opinions don't interest me.' The arrogant note was back in his voice. 'I don't follow the crowd.'

'You lead it, I suppose,' Nita said sarcastically.

'Sometimes.' His eyes dwelt for a long, thoughtful moment on her lips. 'Let's say I take up challenges when they present themselves to me.'

'You've a very high opinion of yourself, haven't you?' she accused him. 'Pardon me if I don't happen to share it!'

'So last night's advances were all part of the act?'

'What do you think?' she taunted him.

There was a wicked glint in his eye. 'If they were, you certainly put a lot of enthusiasm into your work.'

'Misplaced, no doubt,' she seethed.

'Oh, I wouldn't say that.' He gave a faint, reminiscent smile. 'Not from where I was sitting.'

Nita couldn't think of a reply that would flatten him, and if she stayed by his side any longer, she was afraid that she would resort to physical violence. She didn't know what would happen if she slapped his face, but she had a notion that he would retaliate by some means or other if she did. Instead she gave him a cool, remote smile and excused herself to go to the powder room. It was a cowardly retreat and they both knew it, but at least it left her with her dignity intact.

In the confined space of the toilet she adjusted her make-up, combed her hair and held her hands under the cold tap in an effort to cool herself down. What was it about the man that set her temper at danger level, jarring her control of herself and sending it spinning? Whatever it was, it had to be firmly resisted.

Her head was held high as she walked back to her seat, but the defiance in her manner was wasted on Leon Calveto. He had taken advantage of her absence to take some papers from the bulky briefcase that he had carried on board with him, and he now appeared to be completely immersed in them.

Bored with her company, no doubt. Well, two could play at that game, she thought, as she slid past him into her seat, grateful that the space between first-class seats allowed plenty of room to manoeuvre. In the economy section she would have had to squeeze embarrassingly close to him. And, where physical contact was concerned, the further away she kept from Leon Calveto the better.

She sat back in her seat and took up one of her magazines, flipping through it with a careless air. But she wasn't really seeing the fashionable clothes and jewellery that it featured. Instead questions that she had pushed far to the back of her mind and avoided answering rose and confronted her, refusing to be pushed aside.

How long did it take to get over a major heart attack? And, when her father recovered, what then? Would he have to give up his business activities? If he did, what was left for him to do? He would loathe leading the life of a semi-invalid. But perhaps he had no option in the matter.

And where exactly did she fit into the jigsaw puzzle?

Her first instinct when Leon Calveto had broken the news to her was to make for home. She still loved her father, however his feelings for her might have changed. Although he had always been a shadowy, remote parent, she had never ceased to hold affection for him, even in those last bitter days of wrangling before she left when it seemed that they would never agree again.

She was coming home. But to what? And for how long? She didn't know the answers. Her time was her own, of course, now. She had gone over Jeff's head to the manager of the Pink Flamingo, explaining about her father's illness and the need for her to travel home as soon as it could be arranged.

He had given her a sympathetic hearing—which was more, she suspected, than she would have got from Jeff. She had a notion that he might have chosen not to believe her story. It would not have been the first time he had heard the excuse of family illness to cover for some other, less acceptable reason for absence, and, having seen her with Leon Calveto, he would no doubt think the worst.

But the manager had no such misgivings. He had told her to go and pack. He would find a replacement somehow, he assured her. He wouldn't dream of holding her to the week's notice that her contract with the club stipulated. They would manage. It wouldn't be easy to replace her; she had made quite a name for herself in the short time she had been with them. But something would be arranged.

It was much more than Nita had hoped for, and she was grateful for the help. It would have been a miracle if he had offered to keep her place open for her until she was free to come back to them, and Nita wasn't surprised when he didn't. She had the promise of a glowing reference if she ever needed one, which was some consolation. But working regularly and being seen to do so was the best reference of all.

And, for the foreseeable future at least, that was out. Painfully, reluctantly, she severed the connections. She paid her share of the rent of the apartment to the end of the following month, but told Sandy to find someone else to live there with her.

'I can't take it, Nita,' the other girl protested.

'You can—and what's more, you will,' Nita insisted, thrusting the money firmly into her friend's hand. 'Don't be a fool. It'll give you the time to pick someone you really get on with.'

'Well, if you're sure.' Sandy took the bills reluctantly. 'I don't like doing it, though. You may need the money.'

'A highly paid artiste like me? You've got to be joking!' Nita laughed it off. 'I'll be just fine. I'll be able to get a job somewhere if I need to.'

If she was free. But that was something that she wasn't going to let on to Sandy. She didn't know what she might find at home. But one thing was sure: after three years of independence, she wasn't going to accept an allowance from her father. If he offered it, which was doubtful. Well, she had saved a little, and that would see her through for the moment. When it was gone would be time enough to worry about things.

'I guess you're right.' Sandy allowed herself to be persuaded. 'I sure hope your father is O.K. You'll let me know how everything goes, won't you?'

'Of course I will.'

Then the blonde girl brightened and shot Nita a mischievous look. 'What am I worrying for? You're the one Leon Calveto kissed, not me. You'll probably end up marrying the guy and living in idle luxury for the rest of your days.'

'No, Sandy, a thousand times, no! I've told you how I feel about him.'

'And I've told you I don't believe you.'

'Where Leon Calveto's concerned, I'm completely indifferent,' Nita assured her.

'Where he's concerned, no woman could possibly be indifferent,' Sandy had claimed vehemently.

Perhaps Sandy was right, Nita mused. He wasn't the sort of man one could pass by and ignore. Love him or hate him, he left one bruised by the contact.

Would he take that as a tribute? she wondered. Probably only as his due.

His voice, breaking into her thoughts at that precise moment, startled her, and she dropped the magazine that she was holding. It fell to the floor and his tanned, well-shaped hand retrieved it before she had time to move.

'Thank you,' she said automatically. 'What were you saying?'

Leon Calveto wasn't used to repeating himself. Most women hung on his every word, she supposed. He shot her an impatient look that told her more clearly than anything that he would be as glad as she when the journey was over.

'I said we were nearly home now. There's Popocatapetl.' He nodded in the direction of the window.

Nita leaned eagerly forward for a sight of the great volcano, its snow-tipped peak glimmering pink in the last rays of the evening sunshine. And then it was gone, lost in cloud, as the plane circled to make its final descent into the haze of pollution that was Mexico City.

Landing and clearing Customs was quick and trouble-free and, predictably, a uniformed chauffeur was waiting to relieve them of their cases and escort them to a waiting car. Nita couldn't ever imagine Leon Calveto carrying his own bags and joining the usual scrum fighting for taxis.

As they crossed the marbled floor towards the exit doors, familiar sights and sounds came at Nita from all sides. Swarthy Indian faces contrasted strongly with the more patrician features of those of pure Spanish descent. The brightly coloured *ponchos* and *rebozos* that were part of traditional dress vied in colour with the latest in *haute couture* in small groups of people standing around to await arrivals. And everywhere the babble of Spanish accents fighting to be heard above the noise of the loudspeaker announcements that came every few seconds.

The car was a respectable Daimler, solid, but out of character for Leon somehow, Nita thought. She would have imagined him driving something sportier.

But the girl waiting beside it was exactly what she would have expected of him.

She was dark-eyed and dark-haired with a fashionably pale complexion. And she was tiny. Even the ridiculously high heels she wore brought her barely over the five foot mark. Nita had never thought of herself as particularly tall, but beside this girl she felt like a giantess, oversized and ungainly.

She was beautifully proportioned, though, Nita had to admit. Curves in all the right places and an impossibly slender waist. A man could span it with his hands. Nita wondered if Leon Calveto had ever tried. From the way the girl was looking at him, practically devouring him with her eyes, it seemed likely that he could take matters a lot further than that before she called a halt to proceedings.

Not his wife. The slender, perfectly manicured fingers were ringless. But she would like to be—Nita knew that instantly.

'Leon, I missed you!' The girl made the words sound like a caress.

He laughed as he took her extended hands and brushed them against his lips in a gesture that was curiously intimate for all its formality. 'In only three days? That I refuse to believe.'

'You'd be surprised!' She gave him an arch look and laughed too, a girlish, tinkling sound that grated on Nita.

She moved restlessly. From what she knew of the man it would be typical of him to let her stand by his side and listen to another woman throwing herself at him. But it didn't mean that she had to suffer it patiently.

Then he deigned to remember her existence and turned to effect the introductions. 'Juanita Lopez, Mercedes Cardenas. Mercedes is my assistant and right-hand woman.'

Is that what you call it? Nita thought cynically. But their relationship, however close it might be inside and outside the office, was none of her business. She smiled politely at the other girl and muttered the usual words of greeting, the Spanish courtesies drummed into her since childhood coming easily to her tongue.

Mercedes responded in kind, but her smile didn't reach her eyes. There was resentment there. Three days away from her and she's already wondering if he might have strayed, Nita decided. If you set your heart on a man like Leon Calveto, you must be a constant prey to doubts like that, however confident you were of your own attractions.

'I can easily find my own way into town, if you and your—assistant—have other things to do,' she offered.

'That won't be necessary.'

'Are you scared I wouldn't arrive?' she taunted him. 'You needn't worry—having come this far, I'm not likely to turn tail and vanish at the last moment.'

'I don't doubt it,' he said smoothly.

'No? Then what?'

'I intend to see you safely home,' he told her firmly.

Ever the perfect gentleman, she thought, and wondered if he would class his behaviour of the previous night in that category. But then she had been only a girl who sang in a nightclub for a living. To-day she was Diego Lopez' daughter and every inch a lady.

She shrugged and moved towards the car. 'If you're sure——'

'Quite sure. I have no other plans.'

Maybe he hadn't, but she was quite sure that Mercedes had the evening ahead all mapped out, and it certainly didn't run to a threesome. An intimate dinner for two looked more on the cards, to judge from the smart cocktail dress that the other girl was wearing. No doubt there would be time for pleasure after she had been duly delivered to her father. A troublesome package safely off his hands. And he couldn't be more relieved at the parting of the ways than Nita would be.

Their cases safely stowed away, the car was soon speeding towards the centre of the city. The journey would not take long. Twenty minutes, half an hour at most if they were unlucky with traffic. Leon had elected to place himself between the two girls, although his attention seemed more on Mercedes than herself, as he inclined his head frequently in the other girl's direction to catch a series of remarks that were softly spoken and presumably intended for his ears alone.

As the car took a bend and Nita was thrown against him, she felt the strength of his hard-muscled thigh close to hers. It was an unnerving closeness. His particular brand of maleness was a little overpowering at this distance, she thought. She eased herself cautiously away, flinching from further contact and putting her hand unobtrusively on the window rest to avoid the same thing happening again. She saw the faint lift of his mouth as he noted the action, although his interest appeared to be firmly fixed elsewhere.

So her gesture of independence amused him for some reason. Was it the presumption on her part that he might possibly be interested in her when he had someone as stunningly attractive as Mercedes hanging on his every word? Or was he considering the challenge presented by surely the first woman ever to reject what he had to offer?

The car swerved violently, narrowly avoiding a collision with two others whose owners were exchanging angry shouts and gesticulations as they surged on at an erratic rate. Their own driver added to the general uproar with the warning blare of his horn as he accelerated to pass them safely.

'Now I know that I'm back in Mexico,' said Nita wryly. 'Nowhere else in the world do men have the urge to prove their manhood quite so obsessively!'

'Perhaps nowhere else in the world are there men with so much to offer in that respect,' Leon suggested.

'You think so? I'm not so sure.' She looked straight
at him as she spoke, the inference in her words clear if
he cared to pick it up. 'Empty swagger is just that if
there's nothing behind it to back up the claim.'

Their glances clashed and held, but Leon didn't
pursue the subject further. She didn't know whether she
was glad or sorry. Crossing swords with Leon Calveto
was an experience unlike any other, combining fear
with exhilaration.

They were practically at journey's end now and, as
the car turned into the crowded streets of the city
proper, apprehension about what lay ahead replaced
any other thoughts in Nita's brain. Suddenly she wished
that she had more time to prepare herself. How did she
greet the father from whom she had parted in so much
anger? What was she going to say to him?

It was too late to start rehearsing speeches. They were
past the wide square of the Zocalo, dominated by its
magnificent cathedral, and then all the other tourist
sights, familiar to Nita since childhood, were flashing
by. The Palace of the Fine Arts where she had often
seen the Ballet Folklorico perform; Alameda Park with
its quaint globe lamps, glimmering now at dusk; the tall
spire of the Latin American Tower.

They turned into Reforma, the great avenue that is to
Mexico City what the Champs Elysées is to Paris. Nita
glimpsed the monuments to Columbus and to
Cuahutemoc, the last of the Aztec emperors, and the
tall column of the Monument to Independence, topped
by its gilded angel, gazing out over the city, loftily
careless of the packed lanes of traffic that skirted its
base in a never-ending flow.

They took a side road just before they reached it and
drew up outside a tall, modern building, one of the

skyscrapers that were now a common feature of the
city.

The Hotel Cristobal was Diego Lopez' pride and joy,
the centre of his empire and the first of his chain of
hotels to be built to his own specifications rather than
simply acquired and refitted. It was his proud boast
that it had everything to offer those who stayed there,
tourist and businessman alike—luxuriously appointed
rooms, a swimming pool, a sauna, two restaurants, a
coffee shop, a nightclub and an arcade of small
boutiques, ready to sell the casual visitor almost
anything he could ever want.

No trouble had been spared to make the customer
feel loved and wanted. Her father had spent hours
devising improvements and modifications. But, when it
came to his only child, that concern had been sadly
lacking, Nita reflected. The penthouse apartment,
seventeen floors above street level, had been a lonely
place for a child to grow up.

The smartly uniformed porter who stood at the
entrance to the hotel came forward and opened the
door for her with a flourish and a smile. She slid out
with a word of thanks. She didn't know him, but that
was hardly surprising. In three years there would have
been some changes in staff. He didn't recognise her
either. The admiring leer he gave her legs as she got out
of the car would have been carefully suppressed if he
had been aware that she was the owner's daughter, she
was sure.

But he did know the man who followed her out on
to the marble steps and his sudden air of deference
showed all too clearly in what light he held him. Nita
was conscious of a faint surprise. Was Leon Calveto
such a power in the land, then? Or did all her father's

business associates receive this sort of treatment? She rather doubted it somehow.

She turned to him in another effort to rid herself of his company. Surely now he would consider duty well and truly done and take himself off with his girl-friend? But the polite words of farewell that she had carefully summoned up froze on her lips as she realised that he had every intention of accompanying her inside. A door-to-door service with a vengeance! she thought, but said nothing. Protests meant nothing to this man when he had made up his mind and she would only look undignified if she attempted them.

Instead she gritted her teeth and allowed the firm grip of his hand on her elbow as he led her inside after a brief word tossed to Mercedes. Looking back, Nita saw the sour expression on the other girl's face as they left her behind. It was some consolation at least not to have to suffer her company as well.

They crossed the lobby to the private lift that went directly to the Lopez private apartments. Leon ignored the phone that was intended for callers to announce themselves and produced a key from his pocket— another sign of his casual familiarity with the place and one that made her feel strangely uneasy.

As the automatic doors closed on them she freed herself from his grasp in pointed fashion, but said nothing. If truth were told she was almost glad of his presence now. Anything, anyone was a comfort to support her against the moment when she would have to face her father. Her heart was pounding, her hands clammy, now that the time had come.

It was ridiculous to be nervous about meeting her own father. But so many things had happened since the last time they had spoken. She didn't know what kind of man would be waiting for her. A frail invalid or the strong, domineering person that she had always known—which would it be?

The hum of machinery stopped and the lift doors opened on to a short corridor with an apartment entrance at the end of it. Would Leon Calveto have a key for that too? It appeared not. He rang the bell.

'We are expected,' he said as they waited.

He must have telephoned from Miami before they left. It was probably the wisest course. Sudden shocks were the last thing her father needed right now. But it was strange to be treated like a visitor to her own home.

The sound of steps and at last there was a familiar face, older, greyer, with new lines of strain added to the mass of wrinkles that had been there for as long as Nita could remember, but still instantly recognisable.

'Josefina!'

*'Señorita!'*

Nita was over the threshold in an instant, formality cast aside as the housekeeper's arms came out to envelop her in a loving embrace. They were both close to tears.

It was Josefina who recovered herself first, standing back and scanning Nita with shrewd, button-black eyes that never missed anything. 'Let's be looking at you.' She tutted with the fondness of an old servant. 'What have you been doing to yourself, child? Shadows under your eyes and as pale as a ghost! What have you got up to while you've been away?'

As if she had been absent for weeks rather than years! Nita laughed shakily. 'You never did hold with travel to foreign parts, did you, Josefina?' A similar response had greeted her on her return from every holiday she had ever taken. 'But I'm fine, really I am. Just worried about Papa.'

The older woman shook her head. 'It's been a worrying time.'

'How is he?'

'Better every day, thanks be to God.' The housekeeper crossed herself fervently. 'He'll live to be a hundred, you'll see.'

'I hope so. Where is he?'

Josefina smiled reassuringly. 'Waiting for you in his room. And probably cursing me roundly for keeping you talking out here instead of sending you straight in to him. So you'd better go along to him and not waste any more time.'

Nita needed no further bidding. She made her way eagerly towards her father's door, her apprehensiveness forgotten.

'Nita——' Leon Calveto's voice halted her before she had taken two steps.

'Well?' She had completely forgotten about him.

'Go easy with him,' he said abruptly. 'He's had a tough time.'

'I had realised that.'

'See you remember it, then.'

Did he think she was so insensitive? Nita ignored him, turning her back on his tall figure. She gave a brief rap on her father's door and, taking a deep breath, went in.

'Papa?'

'Nita?'

Both voices were strangely uncertain.

'I've come home, Papa.'

'And about time too.' His tone was a pale shadow of its usual strong command.

'Oh, Papa!' she whispered.

He looked different somehow, drained of his vital

energy. He had aged ten years since she saw him last. The dark hair, so like hers, was liberally streaked with grey and his face had lost its ruddy colour. For a moment Nita hesitated just inside the door, then she moved impulsively forward to embrace him and collapse on her knees by the side of the easy chair in which he sat.

'It's been a long time,' he said gently.

'Too long,' she said, blinking furiously to hold back the tears that threatened.

'I thought I wouldn't miss you. But I did.'

For Diego Lopez, the man who had always boasted of his iron control over his emotions, that was quite an admission. He had never told her to her face that he loved her. Perhaps he thought it unnecessary. But now, for the first time, he was letting her know how much he did care.

'I missed you too.' She tried for a lighter note. 'But you didn't need to stage a heart attack just to get me back! A phone call would have done as well.'

He laughed. 'I'll remember that another time.' He sat back in the chair, visibly relaxing, although he retained a tight grip on her hand as if he needed to reassure himself that she was still there.

'I hope there won't be another time.' Nita's voice was low. She didn't want to rake it all up again, but she had to say something. 'What happened three years ago won't happen again. Things should never have gone as far as they did—I realise that now.'

He grunted. 'That's what Calveto said. He told me I was a stiffnecked old fool.'

Trust him to make his views known! But the blame didn't lie all on her father's side. 'And I was a stiff-necked young fool,' she admitted.

'Like father, like daughter. And I always thought you took after your mother.' He was smiling now, pleased at the discovery.

'So did I.' Nita had been reluctant to acknowledge the traits that she shared with her father, but, since she had left home, she had been forced to own to herself that her toughness, her determination to stand on her own feet, her temper when roused, were all qualities that she drew from him, not from her gentle, compliant mother.

'Your mother never minded being told what to do,' he added.

'No.' Her mother had worshipped the ground her domineering husband had walked on. It had never occurred to her to question him. 'But I did. We wanted different things.'

Perhaps they still did. For all the regrets they were uttering over the rift between them there was no indication that there had been a real change of attitude on either side. But it was early days yet. Their new relationship was too shaky, too uncertain to bear discussions of the type that had already brought disaster once. They recognised the fact tacitly and spoke of other things, although Nita could happily have done without Leon Calveto's name being dragged into the conversation.

'What did you make of him?' There was something of her father's old imperiousness in his tone.

She shrugged, assuming a casual attitude that she was far from feeling. Even the mention of the man was enough to make her hackles rise. 'There's hardly been time for me to form an opinion of him. I only met him yesterday.'

'That's twenty-four hours ago.' Diego Lopez gave her a searching look. 'I sized him up in twenty-four minutes, probably less.'

'You're good at making snap judgments,' she reminded him.

'I've had to be.' He didn't contradict her. 'My business life has often depended on it.'

'I suppose so.' It occurred to Nita to wonder what was happening to the business, but she didn't comment on it. She supposed her father's deputy, José Guerrero, would have taken control for the moment. It would be a while before anyone knew whether Diego was well enough to take back command. She imagined it was too soon for doctors to give a verdict on that.

'A sound instinct for character is the best asset a businessman can possess,' her father assured her.

'And what did your instincts tell you about Señor Calveto?'

She already had a shrewd idea. Any man who could call her father a stiffnecked old fool and still remain on speaking terms with him afterwards must have quite a lot going for him.

'He's a young lion. They named him well there. He reminds me of myself at that age. Of course I didn't have his advantages—I came up the hard way, I started with nothing.'

'Yes, Papa.' Nita hid a smile. How many times before had she heard that boast. 'I gather Señor Calveto didn't?'

'No. He comes from a wealthy background. His grandfather built up the family fortune and his father doubled it. They were both very able men. But I think he'll outstrip them both in achievements, given time and opportunity.'

'He certainly seems very sure of himself,' she said. She tried to keep the sour note out of her voice, but failed.

'You don't like him?'

'Do my feelings matter?' she fenced lightly. 'I told you, I barely know him.'

'He's been good to me, Nita. I'd like you to be friends.'

Was it possible for a woman to have a friendship with a man like Leon Calveto? She doubted it somehow. He demanded total capitulation from any female with whom he came into contact. Nita thought of Sandy and her stupidly besotted expression when she spoke his name. She thought of Mercedes Cardenas, hardly able to drag her eyes away from him. Nita told herself that she would rather be dead than let him see adoration for him in *her* eyes ever.

'Nita?'

Her father sounded faintly querulous and she felt suddenly guilty. In his present state of health she should be humouring him, not arguing about something that didn't matter in the least.

'He's been good to both of us,' she said quickly. 'If it hadn't been for him, we wouldn't be talking together now. But there's only one man who matters in my life at present, and that's you, Papa. I want to see you get well.'

He gave her a tired smile and squeezed her hand. She realised now that the interview had taken more out of him than she had imagined possible. She had never known her father ill before. It was a new experience for both of them and one that would take a little getting used to.

'I'll leave you to rest now,' she said. 'Is there anything I can get for you?'

He shook his head as if it was suddenly an effort for him. 'I'll be all right.'

'I'll see you later, then.'

Nita closed the door softly behind her and almost cannoned into Leon Calveto as she turned abruptly round towards the *sala*. She started, her nerves jarring at the sight of him.

'I thought you would have gone by now,' she said ungraciously.

'Without saying goodbye to you?' His eyes mocked her.

'I think I could have survived the experience.'

'How is he?' His head jerked in the direction of the room she had just left.

'Tired right now. He needs to rest.'

'That's only to be expected. It must have been quite an emotional half hour for him.'

'But not for me, of course,' Nita said tartly.

'I didn't say that.'

'You didn't need to. You've made your feelings crystal clear. You think I don't give a damn about my father, don't you? I wonder if the Prodigal Son had the same problem when he decided to come home?'

'Quite possibly, if he overreacted the way you do.' He sounded unmoved by her anger. 'But there's always a chance that I might change my mind about you. Keep trying.'

'I'll see you in hell first!'

Leon didn't waste time on further arguments. Instead, before Nita could guess what he was about, he acted. Strong arms pulled her towards him as effortlessly as a rag doll, and the surprised 'oh' of disbelief that she was about to utter was blotted out by the pressure of his mouth on hers.

There was no defence against that sure, sensual expertise. He knew what a woman wanted. It took only the touch of him to kindle a response. Reason warred with instinct and fought a losing battle as she felt desire flow through her like a warm tide. She couldn't stop herself.

Leon took his time; he could afford to. He knew that he was in total control of her. And, when he drew away from her, it was his decision to do so, not hers. She wasn't capable of conscious thought.

'So you'll see me in hell, will you?' he said with a faint, derisive smile.

Then he turned and left her alone.

## CHAPTER FOUR

NITA was surprised how easy it was to make the transition back to the ways and customs of her old life. She thought and spoke in Spanish again with scarcely a hesitation. She ate the spicy Mexican dishes that Josefina prepared for her without any ill effects whatsoever. She didn't even suffer from the dizziness that the city's mile-high location and pollution-filled atmosphere often induced in visitors and those who had been away from it for any length of time.

She moved back into the room that had been hers since she was a little girl. Somehow she expected all traces of her occupation to have vanished, and she was strangely touched to discover that everything was exactly as she had left it, lovingly cared for by Josefina in the interim.

The first thing she did, even before she unpacked her cases, was to inspect all her treasures. Accumulated and jealously hoarded over the years, there had been too many to take away with her when she left. They filled every available ledge. There was the black paperweight in the shape of a turtle that her father had brought back from some trip or other; the brilliant lacquered box that had been a birthday present from a school friend; a gaudy papier mâché representation of the Nativity with Mary and Joseph in Mexican dress that Josefina had bought for her one Christmas long ago.

And, on the table by her bed, her stylized picture of an Aztec warrior god, reproduced from the carved relief of an ancient temple. His worshippers had offered him warm, still beating hearts as a tribute, hoping that he would give them success in battle, but bloodthirsty or not, Nita had always rather fancied him.

She looked at him critically now. There was something horribly familiar about the arrogant tilt to his head and that firm, sensual mouth. They said that those who were sacrificed to the god gave themselves freely, overcome by the power that he had wielded, but Nita had always been sceptical about that.

But now she wasn't so sure. Hadn't Leon Calveto had exactly the same influence over her? She went hot with shame and fury when she recalled what easy victories he had scored over her, despite her protests. What was it about the man? Pure sexual chemistry, she supposed. It was humiliating to have to admit it, but it was true.

And what was to be done about it? If she couldn't control herself in that sort of situation, it was best avoided. And so was he. She would take the easy way out and make sure that they didn't meet.

In fact, it was not the simplest of paths to follow. Leon Calveto was a frequent and welcome visitor to the apartment, and whoever else was put off with pleas of tiredness or the need to follow doctor's orders, he was always allowed in. His calls did her father good, Nita had to admit. He brought news of a world outside that she knew nothing of; gossip about mergers and business ventures, tales of disasters and triumphs; talk of personalities known to them both. And all of it carefully edited to make sure that there was nothing to upset or disturb the patient.

At first Nita kept to her room when he called, venturing out only when the whine of machinery told her that the lift had taken him down to the ground level again. But her father noticed her absence and commented on it.

'You're always missing when Leon is here.'

He had dropped the formalities, she noticed. He spoke about the man like another member of the family. She wasn't sure she liked it.

'I hadn't thought about it,' she lied quickly.

'I had. You're always on hand to meet other visitors, but never for him.'

Her father's powers of observation were as keen as ever and she cursed them while inventing an excuse. 'He's the only caller who doesn't outstay his time and tire you out. Everyone else would have you dead from exhaustion if I didn't come in and keep an eye on things.'

'Maybe.' But he wasn't convinced.

'And anyway, I'd be bored stiff listening to business talk and you know it. High finance isn't my scene.'

'Leon would know better than to concentrate his attention on business with a lady present,' her father assured her. 'He's not such a boor.'

'No.' Nita's voice was noncommittal. She wondered

how her father would react to some of the things that
she could disclose about the party manners of his
favourite guest. But she said nothing. After all, she
didn't come out of the telling too well either.

She managed to avoid the next two visits by dint of
carefully timed shopping expeditions. And then her luck
ran out. She couldn't dodge Leon for ever, she knew,
and, when the doorbell rang a couple of days later as
she was in the kitchen talking to Josefina, she knew the
moment of truth had come.

'It'll be Señor Calveto, I expect.' Josefina had her
hands full of damp washing that she was unloading
from the machine. 'Could you let him in, *señorita*? We
mustn't keep him waiting.'

'No, that would never do.'

As she went reluctantly out of the room Nita was aware
of the housekeeper's disapproving look following her.
Like every other female between the ages of nine and
ninety Josefina had fallen under Leon Calveto's spell. As
far as she was concerned he had every virtue known to
man. Charm, good looks, money, style, a kind heart: the
list was well nigh endless. And a bachelor too!

It was a great pity that no one besides herself seemed
capable of seeing the other side to the man, Nita
thought as she headed for the front door: ruthless,
domineering, obstinate, arrogant and a lot else besides.

She opened the door to him, pinning a stiff smile of
welcome on her face.

'Well, this is a surprise. What happened? Did you get
tired of finding excuses to avoid me?' The mockery that
was never far from his voice was there in full strength
today.

'Avoiding you?' She gave a careless laugh. 'Why
would I want to do that?'

'You tell me. But you're never around when I'm here, so I drew the obvious conclusion.'

'And what was that?' she asked.

'That you were scared that what happened last time we met might happen again.'

Bang on target as usual. Was there anything he didn't know about the workings of the female mind? Nita doubted it.

He was wearing a cream suit today with a dark shirt and tie. The well-cut trousers hugged his hips and clung to his thighs and the jacket emphasised his breadth of shoulder. He looked wickedly attractive and she was quite sure that he knew it.

*Machismo.* That was the word they used in this part of the world for the quality that Leon Calveto possessed in abundance. That indefinable something that sets a man apart from the common herd—a man's idea of what a man should be. And a woman's too. Despite herself Nita felt her senses stir.

'I've been busy,' she said hastily, neither denying nor confirming his charge. 'When my father came out of the hospital there was a nurse engaged to look after him. But he said she fussed too much and sent her packing after a week, and Josefina's had to manage on her own since then. So I've been giving her a bit of a break and helping out where I can.'

'From hellcat to homebird in the space of a few days?' He sounded lazily amused.

'You find it hard to credit?'

'Well nigh impossible. You must be bored out of your mind.'

Nita was finding it hard to fill her days, if truth were told. Even spending as much time as she did with her father, she had hours to spare every day when he rested.

And Josefina had everything so well organised that there was hardly a useful contribution to be made in that line, although she had just claimed otherwise. She was back to square one, precisely where she had been before she left home—a lady of leisure who disliked the life.

'Don't tell me you care?' she said.

'Is there any reason why I shouldn't?'

She shrugged. 'I'd have thought you were far too concerned with your other affairs to bother wondering whether I'm happy or not.'

'My other affairs?' The dark eyes narrowed slightly as he stressed the final word.

'Your business interests,' she amended hastily. 'What's the matter? Did you think I meant Mercedes Cardenas?'

'She crossed my mind.'

'She would!' Nita snapped waspishly.

'Jealous?' he asked.

'Not in the least. She's very welcome to you as far as I'm concerned.'

He looked amused. 'I'll tell her, shall I? No doubt she'll be relieved to hear it.'

'No doubt. I'm sure she worships the ground you walk on.'

'You think so? It's never occurred to me to ask her.'

'Do you need to?' she said sourly. 'Don't you take female devotion for granted?'

'If I did I'd be at a loss to explain your behaviour,' he drawled.

'I'm the exception that proves the rule.'

'Really?' The corner of his mouth lifted mockingly. 'I don't like making exceptions.'

'I'm afraid you'll have to in my case.'

'We'll see about that,' he said, unabashed. 'And now perhaps we'd better join your father. He'll be wondering what I'm doing to you out here.'

'Doesn't he trust you?' Nita taunted him.

'No Mexican trusts a red-blooded male with his daughter.'

And there was no arguing the fact that Leon Calveto came under that category. She had proof of it. Nita shrugged and led the way to her father's room without further ado.

She hoped that she would be able to make her excuses and leave after a few minutes, returning to the safety of the kitchen until he had gone. But when she started to make noises about leaving the two men to talk together, she found her way blocked. Her father wouldn't hear of it.

'But, Papa, I've so many things to do,' she protested.

'More important than entertaining our guest?' There was reproach in Diego Lopez' voice.

Anything had greater priority than this particular guest, in her view, although she could hardly say so. 'I was settling menus with Josefina——' The pretext sounded thin even as she voiced it.

'Josefina is paid to take care of the day-to-day running of the apartment and to see that it all goes smoothly. If she wants extra help, she has only to say so—I don't want you wearing yourself out.'

'I want to help around the place——'

'And you do, just by being here.' Her father's expression softened. He turned to their visitor. 'You know, Leon, having her home has made all the difference to me.'

'I told you it would.' His glance was enigmatic as it skimmed over Nita's features.

'A man needs his family around him. It's good to be close to someone.' Diego put his arm round Nita's shoulders in a clumsy gesture of affection. 'We've been getting to know each other, my daughter and I, the way we should have done years ago. But there was never time in those days.' He sighed. 'Business, always business—that's all I ever thought about. Take care that it doesn't take over your life the way it took over mine, Leon.'

'I don't think that there's much danger of that,' Leon assured him.

'You work hard. I know the sort of hours you put in.'

The younger man shrugged off the accusation. 'I make time to enjoy myself too.'

'And what sort of pastimes do you enjoy most, Señor Calveto?' As if she couldn't make a shrewd guess! But Nita's voice was politely bland as she put the question to him.

'This and that. It varies according to my mood.' He eyed her lazily. 'I like sport. I have a competitive streak.'

'You mean you like to win.'

'Doesn't everyone?' he asked. 'Isn't that what life is all about?'

'I suppose most men think so,' she shrugged.

'Whereas women prefer to lose gracefully, of course,' he mocked her. 'They accept their role as the weaker sex.'

'Not at all. They usually gain their ends by less obvious means.'

'They're devious.'

'Subtle,' she corrected.

Diego Lopez gave a shout of laughter and threw his

hands up in a gesture of pleasure. 'I think you just met your match, Leon!'

'I never concede a victory while the game continues.' There was a wicked glint in the younger man's eyes. 'If you've no objection, perhaps your daughter and I could pursue the conversation over lunch.'

Diego hesitated, then gave his consent. 'No objection at all. And I'm sure she'd be delighted to join you. Wouldn't you, Nita?'

Nita couldn't think of anything that she would like less. That was why he'd suggested it, she supposed. 'I'd rather stay with you, Papa,' she said carefully.

'Nonsense! You've spent all your time looking after me since you got back. You deserve a little fun.'

Fun! Was that how one described an encounter with Leon Calveto? Not in her book. But there wasn't any point arguing; it was out of her hands. Dutiful Mexican daughters did as they were told. And, this time round, she was doing her best to live up to that standard.

'I'll go and get ready,' she said.

Leon got to his feet to open the door for her and for a second their eyes met, hers registering resentment, his only amused.

He thought that he had scored over her. Well, one encounter wasn't the whole war. Sooner or later, Nita vowed to herself as she went to her room, Leon Calveto would acknowledge that he had bitten off more than he could chew when it came to dealing with her.

In the meantime she had no choice but to fall in with his plans if she wanted to keep her father happy. She frowned at her reflection in a long wall mirror and went to her wardrobe to find a change of clothes. The casual T-shirt and jeans that she was wearing clearly wouldn't do for a lunch date.

How nice it would be to be back in Miami Beach. There almost anything went. Skimpy shorts, low-cut sun-tops, sun-dresses that bared practically all; they were everyday wear and raised no eyebrows. But things were different here in Mexico City, one of the stylish capitals of the world, where formality still ruled when it came to being seen in public.

Nita's hand went out to a chic silk dress. High-necked with long sleeves and a full skirt that swirled elegantly round her legs, it was acceptable in every way—except that its scarlet hue recalled another, less respectable outfit that she had worn in his company.

Not that she cared. She needed the boost that the vibrant colour gave her. She applied her make-up carefully, outlining her lips with scarlet gloss and adding discreet shadow to her eyes. When she returned to her father's room she knew she was looking her best and there was a confident swing to her step.

She paused deliberately in the doorway before going in. If she had learnt one thing from her years in show business, it was how to make an entrance.

'Nita!' Her father's face lit up at the picture she made. 'You look lovely, my dear.'

'Radiant,' Leon Calveto agreed. His eyes mocked her compliance. 'Shall we go?'

She nodded and kissed her father goodbye. 'I'll be back as soon as I can.'

'Take your time. I know you'll be safe with Leon.'

If only she had his faith in the man! she thought wryly. Yet she was conscious of a lift in her spirits as they left the hotel and strolled along in the hazy sunshine towards the Zona Rosa, the fashionable part of town.

It was nice to be going out for a change. And, if her

escort wasn't the one man in the world that she would unhesitatingly have chosen from all others to accompany her, she wouldn't have been human if she hadn't noticed and relished the line of bowing waiters who greeted their arrival at the restaurant and the envious glances that she collected from females at other tables as Leon led her past them en route to their own.

'You approve?' he asked after he had seen her seated and supplied with an aperitif.

'Very much.' She nibbled one of the bite-sized *tacos* that a waiter put in front of her and looked round her in approval at the traditional Mexican decor. The heavy, dark wood of the furniture and fittings contrasted beautifully with the pale, colour-washed walls that were hung with a selection of firearms and touches of colour were supplied by bright posies of flowers on every table. 'In the last few years hamburger joints have been more my scene than exclusive restaurants.'

'And whose fault was that?'

'Oh, mine entirely. I'm not complaining,' she added. 'It taught me how the other half lives.'

'A valuable lesson for a rich man's daughter.'

'A necessary one,' she pointed out. 'It wasn't a case of playing at being poor. When I left home I took nothing with me. I either earned my living or starved.'

'Quite a sharp contrast to the life that you were used to, I imagine.'

'At first,' she agreed. 'But I learnt as I went along. My first jobs hardly paid the rent——'

'And now you're highly sought after and money comes flooding in?'

'Not by your standards, I suppose. And hardly by my father's.' Nita smiled in genuine amusement at the thought. 'But I don't owe anybody anything and I can feed and clothe myself and pay for a roof over my head. And that's not bad in a tough world like show-business.'

'Not bad at all,' Leon agreed.

'Certainly nothing to be ashamed of.'

'Who said it was?' His tone was mild.

What was it about him that put her instantly on the defensive? Nita forced herself to speak calmly, rationally. 'It's on a pretty small scale compared with my father. He made it from hotel clerk to millionaire in ten years flat.'

'So he told me.'

'So he tells everyone. Every interview he's ever given has had banner headlines about his rise from rags to riches. He's always revelled in the fact.'

'But when it comes to his daughter attempting something of the same kind, it's another story. Is that what you resented?'

'I suppose so. He made it so abundantly clear that nothing was too good for his only child. It grated on me.'

'You mean that he acted like every father before him. He didn't want you to have to struggle the way he did. Can you blame him for that?'

'I did once. I don't know if I still do.' Nita wrestled with the problem. 'Money's no substitute for the real things in life.'

'Perhaps not.' The dark eyes were expressionless. 'But I'm sure most girls would have given anything to be in your shoes.'

'That's what Papa used to say.'

'You didn't believe him, of course.'

She paused before answering him, allowing one waiter to fill her glass with red wine and another to serve her with the dish of her choice, beef garnished with tomatoes and peppers and spiced with a rich avocado sauce. She took a few mouthfuls of the delicious concoction and thought furiously as she did so. It was the first time that anybody had forced her to examine her motives for running away, and it was suddenly occurring to her that they weren't as clear-cut and obvious as she had imagined them to be.

'When I was twelve years old my best friend was Maria, the daughter of one of the hall porters at the hotel. She always envied me because I had a wardrobe of pretty dresses and so many books and toys that I didn't know what to do with them all. I don't think she believed me when I said that she had all the things that *I* wanted.'

'And what were they?' he prompted as she paused, lost in memories.

'Love, affection, attention.' She reeled off the list without hesitation.

'I'm sure your father loved you.'

She knew that now; but then she had been uncertain. 'Children need proof that they're loved,' she told him. 'I didn't notice until my mother died. I was eight then and suddenly I felt the cold. Other children had two parents to talk and play with them and take them on holidays, but I only had one, and he was always too busy to be bothered. Sometimes I didn't see him for days on end. He was never there when I needed him—birthdays, school prize-givings, that sort of thing. It hurt.'

'That was hard,' Leon agreed, and she looked at him quickly, expecting to see the usual sarcasm on his face. But, for once, it was absent.

'Being a rich man's daughter isn't easy,' she said. 'The older I got the more I realised that.'

'And the more you disliked the position?'

She took up her wine and savoured its rich, full-bodied flavour. 'Is that so strange?' she asked.

'Not at all. Rebellion is a fairly fashionable thing for those with time on their hands and nothing better to do.'

'I wasn't following fashions,' she protested. 'I had genuine grievances.'

'Really?' That sceptical note was back again.

Nita tossed her head defiantly. 'Yes, really. I don't suppose they featured very much in my father's version of events, if he mentioned them at all.'

'Tell me,' he commanded her.

'You're really interested?' She looked at him, surprised.

'Do I seem so self-centred and uncaring?'

'Not at all. When it suits you, you can be very sympathetic. To my father, for instance.'

'You mean that it hasn't suited me to put myself out in your case?'

'Let's just say that you haven't wasted much sweetness and light on me in the course of our brief acquaintance,' she said dryly.

'We started off on the wrong foot,' Leon reminded her.

'So we did.'

'That doesn't mean we have to go on that way.'

'Don't tell me you're admitting that you may have misjudged me?'

'I'm admitting nothing,' he said coolly. 'Beyond the fact that you show your worst side to me and I react accordingly.'

'So you're willing to concede that I have a better nature than you gave me credit for at first?'

'Who knows what I might believe if you gave me a little encouragement?'

'Encouragement is the last thing that a man like you needs!' Nita shot back at him instantly.

'There you go again, flaring up at nothing!'

'You make it very difficult not to,' she retorted.

'I'm not used to females who bounce back as quickly as you do.' He gave her a sudden smile.

He looked different when he wasn't frowning at her—approachable, charming, totally irresistible. The sort of man one dreamed about. Damn him! She couldn't fight that attraction. She found herself smiling back at him.

'You're as prejudiced as my father,' she accused him lightly. 'He's got old-fashioned views about women and their place in society.'

'Whereas you're all in favour of the Liberation movement?'

'I'm half American, remember? I believe in freedom. And that means that women should decide for themselves what they'd like to do with their lives.'

'And that didn't happen in your case, I take it?'

Nita pulled a face. 'Women don't have careers, according to my father. And certainly not on a public stage. They keep out of the limelight. They get married and produce children.'

'You're against marriage, then?'

'No, not exactly.' Nita hesitated, then went on. 'My father had someone already lined up for me. I thought arranged marriages went out with the Dark Ages, but it seemed I was wrong.'

Leon laughed at her indignation and she registered another involuntary tug of attraction even as she protested, 'It's not funny!'

'No, I suppose not. Did you dislike the man so much?'

'I'd never met him. I never even heard his name. The idea was quite enough to put me off, so I decided that it was time we had a little straight talking, a father-to-daughter chat of the kind that we'd never had before.'

'And where did it get you?'

'Precisely nowhere. I should have guessed as much.' Nita sobered as she thought back to that last, blazing interview with her father. 'It was rather late in the day for Papa to take a crash course in how to handle me. He played the heavy parent and assumed that I would do what he wanted. He misjudged matters. It was quite a shock to him to discover that I could be as obstinate as he was when it came to something that mattered to me.'

'Something or someone.'

Leon's tone was deceptively bland, but it didn't fool her. So he knew the whole story. Her father must have told him everything.

'Yes,' she agreed. 'Or someone.'

'There was a man.'

'Of course there was a man,' she said impatiently, pushing her empty plate aside. 'I was nineteen, and half the girls I was at school with were married and mothers already.'

'And you thought you'd like to emulate them?'

'I thought I'd like to view the possibilities. It would have been unnatural if I hadn't.'

'And the lad you picked on seemed the best available match?'

Nita felt her cheeks grow warm. 'I thought so at the time, but my father didn't happen to agree with me. He told me to give him up.'

'And instead you ran away with him.'

She glanced uncertainly across at him. How could she explain to a man as assured as Leon Calveto? Had he ever been a callow youth infatuated with a girl? Had he ever thought himself in love, only to discover that it was nothing of the kind? She doubted it somehow. His head would always rule his heart, she suspected.

'I loved Antonio,' she said. 'I thought it would last for ever.'

'Nothing is for ever,' he told her. 'Least of all love.'

'You're a cynic!'

'A realist, perhaps.'

If only she had been more realistic about her relationship with Antonio. What had it amounted to anyway? An introduction at the house of a friend. Mutual attraction. Antonio was a year older than herself, tall, broad-shouldered and with the kind of flashy good looks that young girls went for.

And she had been no exception. Inexperienced and naïve, she had been flattered by his attentions. When her father found out about their friendship and tried to put a stop to it, there had been secret meetings and a few furtive kisses and caresses, nothing more. Not enough to know what he was really like. And, by the time she had found out, it was too late.

'He didn't marry you,' said Leon.

'*I* didn't marry him,' she said proudly.

Disillusion had set in almost immediately. It had all been so exciting, planning her escape from home and successfully carrying it off when her father was safely away on a business trip. A new life lay ahead, with the chance to use the singing training that she had received. A career on the stage and a husband by her side to support her.

But feelings of anticlimax had quickly surfaced.

Antonio hadn't seemed quite as attractive in the sleazy hotel room that had been all they could afford in the small border town where they had taken refuge from possible pursuit until their marriage was safely solemnised.

Antonio had been annoyed because she brought so little money with her. He had none of his own and he was depending upon her to supply the deficiency. Naïve she might have been, but it took only a few hours for her to realise that the greatest of her attractions for Antonio was the possession of a wealthy father, who could be talked round to approving his daughter's marriage to a nobody, if matters were presented to him in the right way. For money and money alone, he was prepared to marry her.

'I made a mistake,' she said. 'I lost my reputation—at least by Mexican standards. But fortunately, I didn't commit the ultimate error and marry the man. I found out what he was like in time.'

'Your father was right, in fact.'

'Yes. Not that I was prepared to admit it at the time.'

Leon drained his glass deliberately and set it down. 'You didn't consider going home at that point?'

'What—with my tail between my legs, begging for forgiveness?' Nita laughed shortly. 'No. I've got my fair share of Lopez pride.'

'He would have forgiven you.'

'Yes,' she agreed. 'If I'd said I was wrong to oppose him and run away. If I'd told him that I was truly sorry and promised it would never happen again. But I wasn't, not really. Nothing had changed. I still wanted to be free to make my own decisions about the future. I'd have given up that freedom for ever if I'd tamely gone back at that point.'

'Maybe. So you went it alone?'

'Yes.'

'That was courageous of you.' There was a hint of admiration in Leon's voice.

Nita shrugged. 'I was desperate.'

'So you went north and found work in America.'

'Yes.'

He made it sound so simple, but it hadn't been. The first few months had been the hardest in her pampered existence. She had taken any number of casual jobs to keep herself fed and housed—waitress, laundry-room maid, cleaner, helper in a supermarket stacking cabinets with frozen food.

And, in the evenings, when she had come back from work almost too tired to put one foot in front of another, she had washed and changed and gone the rounds of the all-night diners, truck drivers' stop-overs and the like, looking for a job as a singer and taking anything that she was offered just to get a little experience. She sang for nothing more than her supper on many an occasion.

'It must have been tough,' Leon commented.

She laughed. 'That's the understatement of the year! Yes, it wasn't all roses. But I survived.'

'And emerged from the process a better person, do you think?'

'Tougher, certainly. It opened my eyes to a lot of things.'

'And closed them to others, it would seem.'

'Such as?' she queried.

'Feelings. Emotions.'

'They only make one vulnerable,' she shrugged. 'I prefer to do without them.'

'That's a pity,' he said.

'Why?'

'You must miss out on a lot of worthwhile opportunities.'

'Such as the chance to be another scalp hanging from your belt?' she asked sweetly. 'I think I'll survive the experience.'

'Perhaps.' There was a glint of devilry in his eyes as he spoke. 'You might, however, be persuaded to change your mind.'

'I wouldn't take bets on that,' said Nita.

'Wouldn't you?'

The confidence in his voice scared her.


## CHAPTER FIVE

IN the days that followed Nita's father improved steadily and, for the first time, he ventured out of the apartment for a short walk. But the pleasures of the nearby Chapultepec Park soon palled on him and within two weeks of Nita's return home he was agitating to be allowed to visit the country club that he had always patronised on the outskirts of the city for a game of golf with his cronies.

His recovery was such that his doctor gave his consent, and the outing was successful. It was the first of many. Sometimes the chauffeur drove them out there, sometimes Nita took the wheel. But, more often than not, Leon Calveto found time to take them in his own car.

Thrown into his company with no choice but to suffer it willingly or give offence and upset her father,

Nita made the best that she could of the situation, and since the day that he had carried her off for lunch an uneasy state of truce had existed between herself and Leon.

Uneasy on her side at least. She was wary of him, scared that he might try to implement his threat of making her fall for him. In a way she was almost sorry that she had let him lure her into talking about herself and her past. It had shown him her vulnerable side, and she sensed that he would exploit her weakness to the full if it suited his purposes to do so.

But, without his escort at the country club, she would have spent long, boring hours on her own while her father and his friends occupied themselves on a leisurely circuit of the golf course. The club offered any number of sporting activities to its members, but a woman on her own was not best placed to enjoy them.

With Leon she would stroll round the spacious club grounds, returning to the shade of the members' patio where staff would serve them with cool drinks and savoury snacks while they waited for Diego Lopez and his opponents to join them after the game. They discussed everything under the sun. Leon had firm views on most subjects, she discovered. Art, music, politics, history; he could talk about them all with interest and knowledge.

Often Nita's ideas were diametrically opposed to his and the discussions would be fast and furious. She didn't like the man, she kept telling herself. And she didn't trust him an inch. Yet, in a strange sort of way, she found herself relaxing her guard and enjoying their verbal sparring matches, encounters from which he invariably emerged the winner, but where she often managed to give a good account of herself. Unlike any man she had met before he tested her wits to the utmost, and she found it a not unpleasant experience.

But the man who lay beneath that polished, sophisticated exterior revealed little of himself to her. She knew his favourite restaurants and the sort of films that he liked to see. She knew that he disliked opera because it bored him, although he enjoyed the theatre; the sort of superficial details that she might have discovered about any new acquaintance.

But the real Leon Calveto defied analysis. Whenever she tried to dig a little deeper she found herself up against a blank wall. She suspected it was a deliberate ploy on his part to intrigue her. And if it was, he had chosen the one way that was likely to succeed. She was curious to know what made him tick, and the more he denied her the knowledge the more she delved for it.

'How is it that you're able to get away from the office so much during the week?' she asked him on one such occasion. He said remarkably little about his business activities. She had only the haziest idea of what he actually did.

In slacks and a short-sleeved sweater, unbuttoned at the neck to show a tanned chest, only slightly flecked with dark hair, he looked the picture of casual ease as he walked beside her. He was a long way from the hard-working executive that he was supposed to be.

Her question seemed to amuse him. 'I'm the boss,' he said. 'I don't have to answer to anyone.'

'Except yourself when it goes bust.'

'It's not in any immediate danger of doing that.'

'Thus the idle rich,' Nita observed tartly. 'I didn't think that you were a playboy type.'

'I worked hard to get where I am. Do you grudge me a little time off occasionally?'

'A *little* time off?' Nita queried. 'You've been favouring us with quite a lot of your company lately, haven't you?'

'I haven't heard your father objecting.'

'He doesn't see as much of you as I do, of course.'

Leon gave her a quizzical look. 'Bored with me, Nita?'

Only a man who was absolutely sure of his appeal to women could put a question like that and await the answer with a confident gleam in his eye the way that he was doing now.

'I'm tempted to say yes,' she said dryly. 'Just to wipe that smug look off your face.'

'Trying to dent my ego?'

'An impossible task.'

'I'm glad you realise it. It's always best to accept the inevitable gracefully.'

What exactly did he mean by that? Nita shot him a quick, suspicious glance, but his expression remained bland. 'I don't waste time trying to achieve things that don't really interest me,' she said.

'Like my reformation?'

'That's one of them.'

'I'm relieved to hear it.'

They walked on, taking a path that led down to the small stream that meandered through the club grounds. Trees hung low over the water, providing a welcome and secluded screen from the sun and the wild flowers that had been allowed to flourish there made bright patches of colour against the green of the grass.

At weekends it was a popular spot and was often unpleasantly crowded. Today, however, they had it to themselves.

'Peaceful, isn't it?' Nita stood still, listening to the

gurgle of water as it trickled past. 'And so beautiful.'

'Very.' But Leon wasn't admiring the scenery; he was looking straight at her.

She felt suddenly, strangely jumpy. She went over to the edge of the stream and bent absentmindedly to dabble her hand in the water. How cold it was, although the sun was shining. Quite numbing. Or was that the effect of what she had just heard, catching her off balance?

He stood looking at her, a gleam of something—she didn't know what—in his eyes. Was he mocking or serious? She couldn't tell; she never could with him.

'What's the matter, Nita? Have none of the men in your life ever told you that you look good?'

'Frequently.' She was surprised how cool and steady her voice sounded when every nerve was on edge, sensing danger.

'So why should it throw you when I do the same?'

'It doesn't.'

'No?' He took a step towards her. And then another.

Nita straightened up slowly. If she moved backwards she would be in the water. If she went forward she went towards Leon. Instead she stayed where she was, rooted to the spot.

'You don't have to pay me compliments,' she said.

'No, I don't have to. And I don't have to spend any time with you either if I don't choose to. So why do you think I do?'

'I couldn't say,' she shrugged.

'Not even venture a guess?' he mocked her.

He was close to her now, so close that she could smell the tangy scent of the cologne that he used. She shivered slightly as his arms went round her and pulled her back to him, away from the edge of the bank.

'You intrigue me,' he said.

'Is that all?'

'No, that's not all. But I've always believed actions speak louder than words.'

His mouth claimed hers in the kiss that she had been half dreading, half desiring from the start. She had always known that one day it would not be enough for them just to toss words at each other, and now that day had come. Her lips parted, responding to the urgency of Leon's demands, incapable of resisting him. She let him pull her closer to him, feeling the hard strength of his body against hers as she pressed herself to him.

She wanted him as she had never wanted a man in her life before. She could feel sensation racing through her, stirring her, arousing her to a sudden consciousness of her body and its needs. She made no effort to stop him as his practised fingers sought and found the tiny buttons that fastened the front of her blouse and teased them apart to caress the soft swell of her breasts.

She felt the sudden coolness of the grass against her back as he eased her to the ground and covered her body with his. And then she was oblivious to everything but the touch of him, the hard, taut feel of him as he pressed closer to her, the brush of his lips bringing her further pleasure as they sought the hollow at the base of her throat and then descended to make a lazy exploration of each breast.

She gave a little cry of pleasure as his hands roved over her, seeking out the secret places of her and bringing them unimagined delight. First tentatively, then with increasing boldness, she caressed him too. She had little experience in how to please a man. Instinct and that alone guided her as her hands wandered over him, teasing, stroking, touching. She pushed aside his shirt to run her fingers across the smooth plane of his back, feeling the play of his muscles as he moved against her.

He wanted her—she could tell that from his quickening breathing and the increasing urgency of his movements. He wanted her as much as she wanted him. And he was going to have her, here and now. Then as he held off her, his hand going to the belt of his trousers, the awareness of what she was doing struck Nita with the suddenness of a douche of icy water.

What was she thinking of, to give herself blindly, insanely, to Leon Calveto of all people? There was nothing between them, no finer feelings, no affection, no coming together of hearts and minds. This was an animal attraction, a purely physical coupling that had nothing to do with higher emotions.

'No!' she said abruptly, and tried to push him aside, revulsion suddenly taking hold of her.

'What do you mean, no?' There was passion in his face.

'I don't want to. Let me go!' Nita struggled to free herself.

If he chose to go on, she knew she wouldn't have a chance against his superior strength. For a moment she thought she had left it too late, that she had failed. And then he moved away from her. She could tell from his face the effort that it cost him.

'I'm sorry.'

She mumbled the words. How feeble they sounded! God knows what he made of them as an excuse or apology.

'So am I.' Leon wrenched himself away so that there was a distance between them, his breathing still quick and ragged. 'You picked a fine time to change your mind!'

'I said I was sorry,' she muttered.

'That makes everything all right, I suppose.' His face was a hard mask of anger and frustration.

'No!'

Weakly Nita pulled herself to her feet. He stretched out an automatic hand to help her, but she ignored it. She straightened her skirt and pulled the edges of her blouse together. Her hands shook as she fumbled to do up the buttons, making the task seem endless.

She could feel his eyes on her even though her head was bent away from him. Contempt, rage, disappointment; he must be feeling all those emotions. She was feeling them herself.

She supposed he despised her; in his position most men would feel the same. He thought she was experienced—her every action had led him to believe that she was as eager as he was. And then she had deliberately called a halt to it all.

'There's a name for women who lead men on and then back off,' he snapped. 'If you've tried the trick before, I expect you've heard it.'

He wouldn't believe her if she told him that he was the first man to get that far with her. The first man to make her senses sing, to bring her body alive to that incredible feeling of physical pleasure. Clearly virgins didn't behave in the way that she had done.

'Why?' he asked her curtly.

'Does there have to be a reason?'

'There usually is.'

Nita hesitated.

'Well?'

'We don't even like each other, you and I,' she said. 'That's why.'

'No? I thought we seemed to have developed a

reasonable degree of understanding of each other's needs just now.'

'I didn't mean sexually.'

There was faint derision in his face. 'Oh,' he said softly, 'we're talking about the finer emotions, are we? Love, not lust. Is that it?'

'And if it is?'

'There's nothing wrong with that, if it's what you truly believe.'

'And you think I don't.'

Leon laughed shortly. 'We'll discount Antonio Diaz,' he said. 'Because he was the first man in your life and I'm ready to grant that he turned your head. But are you seriously asking me to believe that you were in love with the man who was enjoying your favours back in Miami? What was his name?'

'If you mean Jefferson Peters——'

'That's the one.' His lip curled contemptuously. 'He didn't appear to be labouring under any delusions about you. In fact he seemed quite resigned to sharing you with anyone else who came along. Are you trying to tell me you loved them all? Either you've got a heart as accommodating as they come or you don't know the meaning of the word.'

'And you do, I suppose?' Her fingers itched to slap his face.

'I've clearer ideas on the subject than you have, I think.'

'If you despise my way of life so much, I'm surprised you bother with me at all,' she snapped.

'I told you, you——'

'Ah, yes—I intrigue you. I'm flattered, of course,' she said with heavy sarcasm.

'You should be. It doesn't happen very often.'

Nita supposed not. Most women would willingly lie down and let him trample all over them on their very first meeting with him. Witness Sandy's reaction to him, for example. The times he encountered opposition must be few and far between.

'What happens when it does?' she asked.

Leon shrugged. 'I let matters take their course.'

'Which is? No, don't tell me, I think I can guess.' Nita ticked the points off on her fingers as she spoke. 'Pursuit, capture, submission, enjoyment and then rejection on your part. Am I right?'

'Clever girl,' he said easily.

'Clever enough not to fall for it,' she told him.

'You didn't do too well on the test run.'

'I'll know better in future.'

'Maybe,' he agreed. He glanced at his watch as if the subject suddenly bored him. 'Time we were getting back to the club-house, I think. Your father should be through by now.'

For all the world as if what had just passed between them had been nothing more than an idle interlude of no importance at all! For him, perhaps, it had been just that. Afterwards, as they sat in the sun and Diego Lopez treated them to a stroke by stroke commentary of the game that he had just enjoyed, Nita sat unnaturally silent, studying Leon and wondering what to make of him. One thing was certain: she would be very unwise to underestimate the man.

'Nita?'

Her father's voice jerked her back to the conversation that had been only a drone in the background of her thoughts. 'What? Sorry, I was miles away.'

Across the table Leon's glance mocked her. 'Your father was asking if we found enough to entertain ourselves in his absence. The time passed very agreeably as far as I was concerned. You weren't too bored, I hope?'

She met his eyes and, against her will, she could feel the faint colour rising to her cheeks at the knowledge that she saw in them. 'I—oh, no,' she smiled brightly at her father, 'not bored at all.'

'You look a bit flushed.' Diego Lopez noted that at least. 'The sun's been quite warm today. I hope you didn't do too much.'

If only he knew exactly what they had been up to in his absence! Not that she intended to enlighten him. 'Perhaps we went a little too far. We won't do it again,' she said firmly. 'I'll see to that.'

The words were spoken to her father, but the message was aimed full and square at Leon. Out of the corner of her eye she caught the younger man's look of amusement. The game wasn't over for him, she could tell. He wouldn't be satisfied until her had her complete capitulation. She was a challenge to be overcome, and he couldn't resist challenges.

With any other man she would have been sure of the outcome of such a contest. Sure because she had dated quite a few men up till now and the end result had always been the same. However pleasant, however attractive they were, when they attempted to steer her towards bed, she rejected their approaches with ease and few regrets. After the disaster of her first love affair she had no intention at all of getting seriously involved again—and sex meant involvement as far as she was concerned.

But Leon was different; she acknowledged that now. One touch from him and her body melted. She had laughed when Sandy talked about the power of physical attraction. 'I couldn't help myself—he was driving me wild.' How often had her friend said that to excuse what was, in Nita's eyes, a casual fling with no genuine depth of feeling. 'What you need is will power,' she had replied then, feeling that Sandy succumbed a little too easily. Now she knew that will power had a way of disappearing when one needed it most. It was no defence at all against Leon Calveto.

Nita braced herself for their next meeting. She would be cool and casual then. She would act as if nothing had happened between them—nothing of any importance, at any rate. But the encounter was some time in coming. Leon had taken off on a sudden business trip, her father told her, and he wasn't sure how long he would be away.

Good riddance, thought Nita, and told herself she could use a respite from his company. As her father's health began to permit a degree of socialising, she accompanied him on his visits to the houses of friends. She was new on the social scene and attractive with it, and the young males of her acquaintance were soon queueing up for her favours.

'Like bees round a honeypot,' Diego Lopez said proudly. 'I always knew I had a beautiful daughter.'

And he wasn't the only man to tell her that. The compliments and invitations flooded in on all sides. She could have been out every night of the week if she had wanted to be. The Nita of three years ago might have been in danger of having her head turned by the attention, but the Nita of today had grown up a little in that respect. She merely laughed and took none of it seriously. Flattery bored her. If truth were told, she preferred Leon's more astringent approach.

She enjoyed herself. Now that her initial anxiety

about her father was being replaced by cautious optimism, she could afford to devote a little time to pleasure. The ceaseless social round would bore her if she knew she had to endure it for ever, but in small doses she found it quite fun. She talked girl-talk with the females of her acquaintance and flirted mildly with the males.

Not one of them put her on her mettle the way Leon did, charging every moment spent in his company with a sort of electricity. Not one of them brought a tingling sensation to her skin when he touched her. And she was glad of it, she told herself. One freak reaction like that was quite enough to try to handle. One night at a party she caught sight of Mercedes Cardenas in the distance. She looked elegant, but down in the mouth—missing Leon, Nita supposed. She would never advertise her feelings for a man as obviously as that.

But she was conscious of a sudden feeling of elation that she found difficult to hide when Leon materialised at her side without warning at a gathering she was attending to celebrate the engagement of an old school friend, the daughter of a successful lawyer.

She had looked for him when she and her father had arrived, a quick, semi-automatic scan of the faces present. Forewarned was forearmed, she told herself, explaining away the action. He must have arrived late and that was how she had missed him. Now her heart missed a beat as she looked at him, lean and dark and dangerous in formal evening dress, the cream of his tuxedo emphasising the deep tan of his face.

Nita was suddenly glad she was looking her best tonight in a salmon-coloured jersey dress whose silky folds clung to every curve of her body.

'So you're back at last,' she said, and could have kicked herself for sounding pleased to see him.

'Have you missed me?' A dark brow rose in enquiry.

'There's hardly been time for that. I've been too busy enjoying myself.' She laughed convincingly. 'You're not the only man in the world, you know, however much it may suit you to behave as if you are.'

He glanced carelessly across the room at a group of young men who were viewing his monopoly of Nita with some gloom. Leon's reputation with women evidently made his own sex treat him with some respect. At any rate, no one was daring enough to come over and interrupt the conversation.

'Is that the competition?' he asked. There was a derisive note in his voice. 'Poor Nita!'

'I told you—I've been enjoying myself.'

And she had. Until he came along and made her realise the difference that lay between the callow approaches of the youths who had partnered her so far this evening and the cool confidence with which he treated her. Leon was a man, not a boy, and the distinction showed in every line of him.

He smiled as if genuinely amused. 'I hope you haven't lost your heart to one of them,' he said.

'And if I have?'

'You'd be making a mistake.'

Not as great as if she lost her heart to him. 'Why?'

'He won't marry you.'

'No?' Nita asked. 'You seem very sure of that.'

'Oh, I am,' he told her softly. 'There are girls a man marries and there are girls he plays around with. And, with your past history, you come very firmly into the second category.' His glance raked over her face, assessing it coolly. 'Although I'm willing to concede that you might give a few ambitious mothers a sleepless night or two, worrying that they might have to welcome a night-club singer into the family.'

He was right, damn him! In the stuffy, ultra-respectable circles in which her father moved, Nita was accepted and welcomed everywhere. Diego Lopez was rich and powerful and greatly respected in the community. But, as a future daughter-in-law, she had a definite question mark over her suitability in the minds of the matrons she had met.

No one had actually said anything to her, but the knowledge was there; she had seen it in their eyes. Every one of them wanted her son to marry a nice girl. Nice girls didn't have a past. They didn't run away from home with a man and then surface three years later without him, still unmarried and apparently fancy-free. Nice girls worked in boutiques or offices or stayed at home until they married. They didn't perform in front of live audiences to earn a living. Nice girls led safe, boring existences.

Nita shrugged carelessly, passing off his remarks as if they meant little to her. 'Perhaps I'm not looking for a husband,' she said. 'Perhaps I'll never marry.'

'No?' he queried. 'That would be a waste.'

'Do you think that I'd make some man an admirable wife, then?'

'With a little effort, yes.'

'On whose part?' she asked. 'Mine, I suppose?'

'Oh, there'd be give and take on both sides, I imagine.'

'You think so?'

She looked over to where the young couple they were fêting that evening stood receiving the congratulations of their guests. Her friend Elena looked radiant enough, her hand proudly possessive as it rested on the arm of her new fiancé. Carlos was a good-looking boy and he came from a good family. He was just twenty-two and going places in the family business.

A very suitable match—the sort of marriage that her father had in mind for her three years ago. Whether it was still what he wanted for her she didn't know. He hadn't confided that much to her yet. Love and marriage were two subjects that they had steered well clear of in their conversations so far, each of them anxious to avoid opening old wounds.

Nita gave a small sigh.

'Do you envy her?' Leon asked abruptly. 'Would you like to be in her shoes right now?'

'I don't know,' she told him honestly. 'Do you think he'll make her happy?'

'Maybe. Who knows? Marriage is a gamble.'

'Is that why you've made a point of avoiding it?'

His expression was unreadable. 'I've been biding my time,' he said.

'Playing the field, you mean.'

'There's no law against that as far as I know,' he mocked her. 'I've been waiting for the right girl to come along.'

'And have you found her yet?'

'I narrowed it down to a short list of candidates recently.'

'A practical solution to the problem, if ever I heard one,' she said tartly.

'I'm a practical man,' Leon shrugged.

'Let's hope that, when you've made your final selection, she doesn't turn you down.'

'Oh, I don't think she'll do that.'

Neither did Nita. No one would let a man like him slip through her fingers when he was offering marriage—no one in her right mind, that was. He would be the catch of the season, she was sure.

'I hope you'll invite me to the wedding,' she said. 'I'd like to see the superwoman who takes you on.'

'You think it would take a saint to put up with me?'

'Don't you?' she countered.

There was a sudden wicked light in his eyes as he glanced down at her. 'Virtuous women bore me. I was thinking more along the lines of a fellow sinner.'

Nita wondered who on earth he had in mind. Surely not Mercedes? But before she could pursue the subject further, the lights dimmed and the band that had been assembling at the far end of the room burst into the opening bars of a popular tune and Elena and Carlos took to the floor amidst loud applause to start the dancing.

'I think that safely kills off conversation for a while,' Leon said, and she couldn't tell whether he was glad or sorry. 'Dance with me, Nita.'

It was a command, not a request, but for once it didn't occur to her to oppose him. Instead she let him sweep her on to the floor with the other couples. They danced apart and then, as the catchy beat of the first couple of numbers was succeeded by a slower rhythm, he pulled her into his arms and held her closer to him.

She was tense at first, holding herself rigidly in check as she moved against him, scared of what might happen if she let herself go.

'Loosen up,' he murmured in her ear, pulling her still closer. 'You're as stiff as a board!'

She was being foolish—after all, he couldn't make love to her on the dance floor. She abandoned herself to the music, the fluid movements of her body matching themselves exactly to his, and then discovered her mistake as she felt the now familiar response that only his physical presence seemed to stir in her.

It was what she wanted, if she was honest enough to admit it to herself. It was what she had been wanting all week while Leon had been away from her. As she abandoned herself to the sensual pleasure of him moving against her she knew it was madness, but she didn't care. Nothing mattered except the tide of feeling that carried her along. Dimly, in the background, she was aware of the music, responding automatically to the beat. But other things overshadowed it: the burning touch of his hand through the flimsy material of her dress; the strong, steady beat of his heart against her breast; the slight roughness of his cheek as it brushed against hers.

Leon didn't release her when the music stopped briefly and there was a general change of partners all around them. Nita stood in the circle of his arms, incapable of movement, while Leon looked down at her with faint amusement. He knew exactly what effect he was having on her and he was relishing it, she thought, trying to rearrange her dazed features into a semblance of normality.

'Having fun?' A high, bright voice behind them broke the spell.

It was Mercedes, soignée and sexy at the same time in a low-cut dress of swirling green chiffon, her hair elaborately pinned and coiled. There was a smile on her face, but it didn't reach her eyes. They were as cold and as hard as jet. Nita felt ridiculously guilty, almost as if she had been caught committing a crime of some kind. No doubt that was how the other girl saw it.

'I thought you were still in Cuernavaca. You didn't tell me you'd be here tonight.'

Her tone held an accusing note, one that her partner, a pleasant enough young man, clearly registered. He looked uncomfortable and shuffled his feet, evidently recognising the fact that he was very much an also-ran as an escort when it came to competition with Leon Calveto.

'If I'd been in need of your services, no doubt I would have got in touch.'

The ice in Leon's tone made it quite clear how he felt about being taken to task in public, and Nita felt almost sorry for the other girl as she saw the dull tide of colour that stained her cheeks. And then the music started again and Leon pulled her away from the other couple with a brief nod of acknowledgment to Mercedes' partner, leaving him to pick up the pieces as best he could. Nita didn't envy him the task.

'You weren't very nice to Mercedes,' she ventured.

'I don't like possessive women.' He eased her towards him again, moving in time to the music.

'But surely Mercedes——'

'Forget Mercedes,' he said. 'She's not important.'

'No?'

'No.' His lips nibbled her ear, distracting her attention. And it didn't seem worth arguing about any more.


## CHAPTER SIX

'I'LL be out tonight, Papa, if that's all right with you.'

'Off gadding again?' Diego Lopez put aside some papers that he was studying in the *sala* and looked up as his daughter entered the room some days later.

'Would you rather I stayed in and kept you company?' Nita glanced anxiously at him. 'Are you feeling O.K.?' The doctor had confirmed that he was well on the road to recovery, but he still had his off days when he was obliged to take things easily, and Nita didn't like to be away from the apartment at such times in case he needed her.

'Stop fussing—I'm fine. And only too glad to see you getting out and enjoying yourself instead of being stuck indoors running round after me.'

'I thought that was what womenfolk were for? Don't tell me you've changed your tune at last?' she teased him. 'Anyway, I like being with you. It's no great hardship spending a bit of time with you, you know.'

She wasn't lying to him. She did enjoy the hours they spent together. Diego Lopez was more relaxed these days, more mellow and much easier to talk to. They were alike in many ways, she and her father, and they were discovering common interests and enthusiasms all the time.

She had no doubt at all that she had done the right thing in coming home. She missed the free and easy life in Miami. She missed her friends there, particularly Sandy. More than anything, she missed her singing. She still didn't know when, if ever, she would be able to pick up the threads of her career again; it was too early to think about that possibility just yet.

But it was worth any amount of sacrifice to feel that at last she was achieving some kind of real relationship with the father she had never properly known or understood. And, for his part, Diego Lopez seemed equally grateful to have been given a second chance, an opportunity to heal the rift between them for all time.

'Who's the lucky man this time?' he asked her now.

'Leon. He has some friends in town that he's taking to the Sound and Light show out at Teotihuacan. I thought it was a bit of a tourist trap and I always avoided seeing it, but he says it's quite a spectacle and he thought I might like to go along with them.'

'Leon, huh?' Diego Lopez' glance was shrewd. 'You've been seeing quite a lot of him lately.'

'Do you mind?' Nita was aware of the defensive note in her voice.

He gave her a wry look. 'Aren't you going to tell me you're old enough to choose your own escorts now?'

'Old enough to realise that I can make mistakes about people as easily as the next person.' Nita pulled a face. 'I've been wrong in the past and you've been right. I'm doing you the courtesy of consulting you this time.'

'So, if I tell you to drop him, because I think he's no good for you, you'll obey me instantly.' There was a twinkle in her father's eye.

'He won't see me for dust,' she promised, laughing. 'I'm a dutiful daughter now.'

'When it suits you.' But there was only affection in Diego's voice. 'Go and enjoy yourself. You won't come to any harm with Leon.'

How little he knew! Since the evening of Elena's engagement party she had been fighting a desperate battle with herself. She wasn't going to give in to Leon, but slowly, inevitably, he was eroding her defences. And making no secret of his intentions. Tongues had wagged after Elena's party when he had danced every dance with Nita, and he had left at the same time as herself and her father as if the evening held no joys for him if he was to be deprived of her presence.

At least one of the young men who had professed

interest in her had openly expressed the hope that he wasn't poaching on another man's preserves.

'I wouldn't want to offend Señor Calveto,' he told her earnestly. 'If he's taking an interest in you—that is—I——' He grew scarlet and flustered in an attempt to explain. 'I mean——'

'I know exactly what you mean,' Nita said coldly. The king of the jungle had staked his claim and lesser lights were terrified of standing between him and his prey. 'When I want to stop seeing you, I'll tell you. You needn't look to Señor Calveto for advice.'

'Yes—no.' He had been overcome with embarrassment at his lack of tact and she had felt sorry for him in the end. But he hadn't invited her out again.

'I don't belong to you, you know,' she told Leon sharply one evening when he arrived at a charity cocktail party that she was attending on her father's behalf and the youth that she was talking to made a discreet but obvious withdrawal only moments after Leon reached her side.

'Not yet, no,' he agreed.

'Nor ever will do.'

His eyes narrowed as he glanced down at her. 'If you're so sure of that, what's the problem?'

'You're scaring everyone else away.'

He looked amused. 'It's not deliberate, I assure you.'

No, he didn't have to say or do anything to make his interest in her obvious; it was just tacitly understood. Nita thought back to a story book that she had had as a little girl. Full of animal pictures, it had offered observations on the natures of the beasts it showed. She remembered the lion, tossing its splendid mane. And underneath the sentence had read, 'Monkeys hunt in packs; lions walk alone.'

And that was what Leon was doing. Slowly, determinedly stalking his quarry, waiting for the right moment to spring and secure it for himself.

'Stop playing with me, Leon,' she said crossly. 'I'm not interested.'

'Aren't you?' he mocked her. 'If you really want to be rid of me, you only have to say no and mean it. I'm not that insensitive, I hope.'

He wasn't insensitive at all, that was the trouble. He was alert to every feeling that went through her, every response that she made to him. And he knew that she hadn't the strength to send him away.

She wasn't going to get involved with Leon Calveto, she told herself. He was just a temporary presence in her life—mentally stimulating, physically exciting, but, above all, transient. Mercedes was one stray fancy, now she was another. And his intentions were strictly dishonourable. To view them in any other light would be the mistake of the century. He had as good as told her so.

She knew it all. She had been over it in her head a dozen times and more. Yet she couldn't stop seeing him, couldn't turn his invitations down. As she dressed for the evening ahead Nita saw her glow of anticipation reflected in the mirror and cursed herself for letting herself get excited. What would Leon make of her flushed cheeks and over-bright eyes? The knowledge that he was close to getting his way with her, she suspected. Thank goodness for the outdated Mexican social code which frowned on anything but double-dating for unmarried girls! Old-fashioned and stuffy, she had called it once, but now she was almost glad of the protection it gave her.

The doorbell rang promptly at seven as she was still

getting ready. Unlike most of her fellow-countrymen, Leon was invariably punctual for his appointments and he disliked being kept waiting.

Nita gave a quick, critical look at her reflection and decided that she would pass muster. She was wearing a vivid turquoise skirt teamed with a cream blouse, heavy with embroidery in the same colour, and round her neck she had clasped a turquoise chain, a souvenir of a trip she had once taken to Navajo Indian country. Her hair fell loosely over her shoulders: she had no intention of trying to ape Mercedes' sophisticated coiffures.

She picked up her handbag and a light shawl and left the room hastily. As she expected, Leon was with her father. The two men were deep in conversation, but looked up when they heard her at the door.

'I'm sorry to keep you,' she said politely.

'You were worth waiting for.'

The standard reply, but the lazy way that he studied her from top to toe, taking in every part of her, was far from conventional behaviour. With Leon a woman was never in any danger of forgetting her femininity; he was all appreciative male.

She wasn't going to let him get her flustered. She gave him a cool, poised look. 'Shall we go, then?' She walked over to her father and bent to kiss his cheek. 'You're quite sure you'll be all right on your own?'

'Quite sure,' he told her. 'Josefina is here if I need anything. Anyway, I've got my lawyer coming round to talk a little business with me tonight, so you needn't think I'll be sitting here on my own.'

'Business? But, Papa, you know what the doctor said——'

'The doctor's an old woman,' Diego Lopez grumbled. 'And you're hand in glove with him.' He registered the worry on her face and made haste to reassure her. 'It's all right, I'm not going to overdo it. I'll take care.'

Nita frowned, still unconvinced. 'Is that a promise?'

'Yes, it's a promise,' he agreed with mock resignation. 'That's daughters for you, Leon! Give them an inch and they take a mile. They run your entire life for you, if you let them take over.'

'And don't tell me that you aren't enjoying every minute of the process!' the younger man replied, and there was general laughter.

They took their leave then. Time was passing and they still had to collect Leon's friends from their hotel. They were a married couple, he told her, Emilio and Maria Moreno, and the trip to the capital was in the nature of a celebration for them.

'Maria's doctor has just confirmed that she's pregnant. They've been married for nine years and trying for a family for almost as long. Naturally they're over the moon at the news.'

'I can imagine.'

The Morenos were ready and waiting in the foyer of the hotel. Maria was an attractive, bubbly brunette in her late twenties. Her husband was a few years older, plump and balding, with a pleasant, open face. Nita took to them both immediately. Then, introductions made, they were soon under way again, heading out towards Teotihuacan.

The Morenos had been in town only two days, but already they seemed to have visited many of the sights, Nita discovered.

'Those beautiful murals in the National Palace, the Basilica of Guadalupe—that was wonderful, wasn't it; Emilio?—with that picture of Our Lady that they say appeared on a peasant's cloak all those years ago.'

Maria ticked them all off on her fingers. 'And last night we saw the Ballet Folklorico—that was marvellous!' She went on with hardly a pause for breath. 'Then today we went to Chapultepec Castle—one of the guards there tried to chat me up when Emilio wasn't looking. He was furious when he saw what was going on, weren't you, love? And then we saw the Museum of National Anthropology. Emilio is a bit of a culture vulture, you know. By far the nicest museum I've seen, though—displays everywhere and lots of nice seats around for when you get tired of walking.'

'Which Maria did in the first half hour,' her husband said teasingly. 'She ended up in the coffee shop inspecting the cream cakes.'

'Getting my strength together.'

'I was the one who needed to do that,' Emilio argued, pulling a face of mock horror. 'After lunch she took me shopping. You should have warned me, Leon. I think we went into every boutique in the Zona Rosa. You wouldn't think we had shops at home, the way she was carrying on!'

'Oh, the shops!' Maria sounded rapturous. 'I could have spent all day in them!'

'You very nearly did,' her loving husband pointed out. 'As well as most of my money.'

'Men!' Maria gave him a withering look. 'As if one could expect them to understand! Shopping is one of the few pleasures women have in life, isn't it, Nita? Deprived and downtrodden as we are, grant us a few happy hours.'

'You certainly had those,' Emilio interjected. 'I'm the one who suffered.'

'Rubbish, you enjoyed every minute.' She kissed him on the cheek. 'Didn't you, darling?'

'If you say so.'

The look he gave her made it quite clear how much she meant to him. Emilio obviously doted on his wife. His eyes rarely left her face. And, for all her talk of his supposed ill treatment of her, there was no doubt that she felt the same way about him.

That was how a marriage should be. Nita felt a sudden pang of envy. Would she ever achieve that kind of idyllic relationship with anyone? She found her eyes straying to Leon and pulled herself up sharply. He was the last man on earth that she could ever imagine lavishing devoted looks upon her!

In such lively company the journey passed quickly and the thirty or so miles to Teotihuacan were soon covered. Nita had seen the ruins, remains of an ancient ceremonial centre built by the earliest inhabitants of Mexico, before. But that had been by day. At night the floodlit shapes of the towering Pyramid of the Sun and its smaller companion, the Pyramid of the Moon, had an even greater majesty about them. As they took their seats in the spectators' grandstand overlooking the so-called Street of the Dead the atmosphere of the place reached out to them all, and even Maria's bright chatter dimmed slightly. Nita shivered.

'Cold?' Leon asked. He had been right beside her as they had walked up the steep stone path leading to the ruins, his hand firm on her elbow, guiding and directing her on the uneven surface in case she should stumble, while Emilio performed the same service for Maria.

'A little,' she admitted. The thin shawl that she had with her wasn't really adequate out here in the fresh air of the countryside. Perhaps she should have taken advantage of the chance to hire one of the blankets that were being hawked back at the entrance gate. 'But mainly awestruck.'

'The place where men become gods. That's what they called it, you know.' He looked across at the Pyramid of the Sun, his eyes narrowed against the cold brilliance of the floodlighting. 'One can almost believe it sometimes.' For a second his face was remote, expressionless. Then he glanced at her again. 'The awe I can't dispel, and I'm not sure that I want to try. But the cold——' He broke off to shrug off his jacket in one lithe movement and draped it round her shoulders. 'Is that any better?'

The warmth of his body still clung to it, and Nita hugged it to her, suddenly aching for a closer contact. 'Much better, thank you. But won't you be frozen?'

'I don't feel the cold,' he said.

'You're lucky.'

'Yes.'

He turned away from her to answer some question from Maria on his other side, and Nita sat silent, lost in thought. No, Leon didn't feel the cold. He didn't seek the warmth of a close emotional tie, such as Emilio and Maria shared. What you never had, you never missed, so people said. But it wasn't true in her case. All through her lonely childhood she had been looking for love.

And what had that search brought her? Disillusionment over Antonio, estrangement from her father for all this time, and a useless hankering for something that was probably beyond her reach: a man who could satisfy her on every level: physical, emotional and mental. Perhaps Leon's practical approach to relationships did make more sense.

The light changed then, bathing the pyramids in a

warm, fiery glow as the spectacle began, diverting Nita's mind from her problems. For a while the ancient stones came alive as music, voices and the ever-shifting colours, now red, now green, now icy blue, focussed on them, combining to tell the story of the people who had built this place and the beliefs that they had harboured.

Even the names of the gods that they had worshipped cast a spell. Tlaloc, the rain god; Coatlicue, mother of gods and men and mistress of death; Huitzilopotchi, the god of war; and, most famous of all, Quetzalcoatl, the plumed serpent and bringer of civilisation.

For a brief enchanted hour their deeds echoed round the temples that had been built in their honour, bringing it all alive again to those watching in the dark. And then it was over and the harsh floodlights were back again, the magic set aside for another evening.

All over the grandstand people were coming back to reality, complaining about the cold and their cramped limbs, grumbling about the time it would take to get home again. At the exits taxi drivers claimed their fares and coaches rumbled in to pick up groups of tourists.

Their party headed for a restaurant that Leon knew a few miles distant. It was only fifteen minutes' drive away, and the warmth of the welcome they were given dispelled the chill of the night air. Reluctantly Nita restored Leon's jacket to him with a whispered word of thanks and then went with Maria to the ladies' room so that they could restore some order to their windblown appearance.

'That was terrific, wasn't it? I wouldn't have missed it for anything,' the other girl said as she tugged her comb through her tangled hair and tried to arrange it neatly. 'It was good of Leon to take us. But he's like that, isn't he? Such a kind man.'

'Yes,' Nita agreed colourlessly. It wasn't a description that came instantly to mind. But she couldn't judge his treatment of others by his attitude to her.

'And gorgeous with it! He's got enough charm to sink a battleship, I always tell him. If I wasn't blissfully happy with my darling Emilio I'd be madly in love with him myself.' Maria dabbed powder on her nose and inspected the result. She sighed. 'But he wouldn't be remotely interested in an old married woman like me. He only has to crook his little finger and some super young thing comes running up adoringly.'

'Yes, they do, don't they?'

'Oops! Sorry.' Maria clapped her hand to her mouth. 'I put my big foot in it again, didn't I? Emilio says that I've less tact than a whole herd of stampeding elephants.'

She looked so comically contrite that Nita couldn't help laughing. 'It's all right.'

'Is it?' Maria sounded doubtful. 'I saw the way he was looking at you. He fancies you, doesn't he?'

Was it that obvious that he had designs on her? 'I know what Leon's like,' Nita said. 'I've got more sense than to get involved with him, I hope.'

'I hope so too.' Maria shot her a sharp glance. 'If you have, you'll be the first one ever. I've known him ten years—he was best man at our wedding—and I've lost count of how many women there've been. He changes them the way other men change their shirts. But that doesn't seem to stop them queueing up to be next in line. They can't seem to help themselves.'

'I can.' Nita spoke as much to herself as to Maria.

The other girl gurgled with laughter. 'Poor Leon! Does he know what he's up against?'

'I've told him so.'

'You're playing with fire there. Be careful, Nita.'

As if she didn't know it. Nita gathered up her bag and they went to join their escorts. She studied him under her lashes as they all took their places at the table and was annoyed at the way her senses stirred uncontrollably as she did so. What chance had she of resisting him when her body seemed to be fighting on his side? His eye caught hers and a dark brow lifted sardonically as if she had revealed the struggle that was taking place within her. Damn the man! Nita forced her glance away and made an effort to involve herself in the conversation.

Not that it was difficult. Maria's lively chatter was hard to resist and her husband, although quieter, displayed a dry sense of humour that was equally attractive in its way. Nita discovered that he owned and ran a tourist agency in their home town of Merida.

'You've never been there?' He shook his head in disbelief at her admission. 'You must come. The Yucatan is the jewel in Mexico's crown, the best part of the country. We have everything there—great pyramids built by the Maya people as impressive as anything we saw tonight at Teotihuacan. And then there are the resort islands off the coast. Cancun and Cozumel are within easy reach of us, and lots of fashionable people prefer them to Acapulco these days. You can go swimming, snorkelling, fishing, looking for shells. And Merida itself is a gem of a place. Marvellous colonial atmosphere——'

'You've sold it to me,' said Nita, smiling at his enthusiasm. 'If your sales talk is as good to your customers, business must be booming!'

'Not bad. Not bad at all.' Emilio was modest about his success. 'And Maria is a wonderful help to me. She

supervises the office work and deals with the bills while
I enjoy myself alongside the drivers, taking the tours
out and showing our visitors the wonderful countryside.
I'd be nothing without her.'

'You'll have to learn to manage when the baby comes
along. I can't see myself organising feeding time with
one hand and booking tours with the other,' Maria
warned him.

He waved that aside. 'For a time, maybe. But then
it'll be a family affair. Moreno and Son—I can see the
sign now.'

'Don't count your chickens too soon,' his wife chided
him. 'It might be Moreno and Daughter, you know.'

'Son, daughter—what does it matter so long as it's a
healthy child?'

'Let's drink to that.' Leon signalled to the waiter and
champagne arrived at the table, cold and bubbly,
frothing in their glasses as it was poured out. He held
his aloft and offered a toast. 'To parenthood.'

'When are you going to try it for yourself, Leon?'
Maria asked him slyly after they had drunk.

'Parenthood?' He threw her a wicked look. 'Doesn't
marriage come first?'

'You know perfectly well what I mean.'

'Maria——' Emilio said warningly.

'Well, he does.'

'Maria never gives up. Having found matrimonial
bliss herself she never tires of recommending it to other
people,' Leon told Nita with a brief laugh. 'And I make
the same answer every time she brings it up. I tell her
that if she can guarantee me a lifetime of happiness
along with the marriage lines, I'll head for the altar
quite willingly.'

'You can't guarantee anything in life. You should

have learnt that by now,' Maria scolded him, half joking, half earnest.

'Perhaps that's why I stick to the areas that I know I can control successfully.'

Maria groaned. 'Like business, I suppose. I thought we'd get on to that some time or other!'

'It goes a fair way to keeping me happy, Maria. Are you going to grudge me that small satisfaction?' His eyes danced with wicked lights.

'You're never satisfied!' But the other woman laughed. 'Honestly, Nita, these business tycoons are impossible! He has a property empire that covers practically half the country, but that's not enough for him—Oh no. He has to have fresh worlds to conquer. He was telling us on the phone this morning that he'd just swung the biggest deal of his life, acquired a whole chain of hotels to play about with. But is he satisfied? No. By tomorrow morning he'll have his eye on something else.'

'You may be right.' Maria's vehemence seemed to amuse him. He took another drink of champagne. 'Ambition's a hard mistress. One moment you think you have everything that you could possibly want and the next——' He paused.

'And the next?' Maria prompted him.

'The next moment you realise that it's not enough,' he said deliberately. 'There's always another challenge to be overcome.' His gaze rested for a second on Nita, the meaning in it unmistakable.

She felt the colour rise to her cheeks and hoped the others would put it down to the heat of the room. 'One day you'll meet your match,' she said.

'Perhaps.' His eyes held hers, dark and compelling, then he turned away. 'In the meantime, Maria, you'll just have to keep on nagging at me and hope that I'll reform my wicked ways some time in the near future.'

'That's usually how she gets results,' said Emilio, and amidst the ensuing laughter and Maria's indignant refutation of the charge, the discussion moved into other channels.

Time passed quickly and Nita was surprised to look around her and discover that they were practically the only people left in the restaurant. Her watch showed her that it was after midnight. It was nearly one in the morning by the time they reached the Morenos' hotel.

'It's been a lovely evening, Leon. Thank you.' Maria held out her hand to him and then turned to Nita while the two men had a final word. 'I've so enjoyed meeting you.' She kissed Nita affectionately. 'I hope it's not long before we see you again. If you can spare the time, come and visit us. We'd love to show you the Yucatan.'

'I'd like that,' said Nita, and meant it. After only a few hours in the other woman's company, she felt as if she had found a friend.

'In the meantime, take care of yourself.' Maria's voice dropped conspiratorially. 'Remember what I told you about Leon. I can see a predatory gleam in his eye when he looks in your direction. He——'

'Maria?'

Emilio summoned her at that point, so Nita never heard what further advice she had to offer. There was a flurry of goodbyes and then she was alone in the car again with Leon, speeding through the dimly-lit streets back towards the Hotel Cristobal and her father's apartment.

'I liked your friends,' she said.

'Yes, they're a nice couple. Maria talks a bit too much, as you no doubt noticed, but she's very goodhearted. I've known them both for years. In fact, I was——'

'Best man at their wedding. Yes, she told me that.'

'Did she indeed?' In the half light she saw faint amusement in his face. 'And what else did she confide in you about me?'

'Who says she confided anything?'

'Call it masculine intuition,' Leon said cynically. 'I'm one of her favourite talking points among her female acquaintance. She's been trying to marry me off for years—I've lost count of how many friends and relatives of hers have been paraded hopefully in front of me on the occasions when I've visited them.'

'Christians thrown to the lion?'

'Something like that,' he agreed calmly. 'They certainly embraced the venture with some fervour!'

'I can imagine,' Nita said darkly. 'And you didn't take to any of them? You amaze me!'

'I took to any number. But I wasn't prepared to sign on for a life sentence.'

'Is that how you see marriage?'

'It's what it turns out to be in most cases.' He was silent for a moment as he negotiated an overloaded lorry that was hugging the centre of the road in front of them, then continued, 'With the right woman, of course, a man is a willing prisoner. Or so Maria reliably informs me.'

'You don't believe her?'

'Do you?'

'I don't know. It's what every woman hopes for, at any rate,' she said.

Leon laughed briefly. 'There's usually quite a large gap between expectation and reality.'

'And that's the woman's fault for expecting too much, I suppose.'

'I didn't say that.'

'You didn't need to.' She had heard it in every arrogant note of his voice. 'It's what you think, isn't it?'

'It's usually the female sex that asks for the moon and then cries when it isn't available.'

'Whereas men are more realistic, of course,' she said sarcastically.

'They make the most of what comes their way.'

'A sound doctrine.'

'I'm so glad you agree with me.'

They were nearly at the hotel. Leon had just turned into the narrow side street that led up to it, but, instead of driving on, he swung the car suddenly towards the kerb and brought it to a halt by the sidewalk.

'What—what are you doing?' Nita asked.

'Practising what I preach,' he said as he reached across for her and pulled her into his arms.

She tensed, prepared to struggle, although she knew it would be a hopeless contest. His superior strength would overpower her instantly. But this time he chose a more devastating weapon. It was his gentleness that conquered her in the end. The caressing movement of his thumb against the soft skin of her upper arm, the feather-light touch of his lips against hers, made her tantalisingly aware of him, incapable of resistance.

It was a slow, insidious invasion of her senses. Apprehension faded, to be replaced by excitement and growing desire. She could feel a glow spreading through her, a mindless ecstasy that banished independent thought and made her strangely reluctant to do anything other than give herself up to the sheer erotic pleasure of the moment.

She wanted Leon as a parched plant wants water. She could feel herself coming alive as his hands made a leisurely exploration of her body, teasing, stroking, arousing her to fever pitch, her breath coming in quick gasps as sensation pulsed through her. She pressed herself closer to him, revelling in the hard strength of his body against hers.

'I want you, Nita.' The words were a low, urgent mutter as his mouth found hers again in a long, devouring kiss. She felt a shudder run through him. 'God, but I want you!'

Nita said nothing, but her body gave its own answer, her willingness all too apparent, her arousal complete. She wanted him to go on, to give her the final fulfilment that her senses craved. Nothing else mattered.

When he put her roughly aside and turned away from her, she was conscious only of that inner voice, begging, pleading for him to continue that mind-bending rapture.

'Leon?' Her voice broke as she spoke his name. She stretched out a hand to him, but he pushed it rudely away.

'Don't touch me, Nita, or I won't be responsible for what happens next,' he warned her in a ragged tone that told her how far he was from his usual cool control of himself.

She felt as if she had suddenly been dropped from a great height. Her head reeled with reaction.

'Leon, why?' she asked after a moment.

In the darkness she couldn't see his expression, only the dim outline of his head and the rapid rise and fall of his chest as he fought to steady his breathing.

He didn't answer immediately and she thought he hadn't heard her. Then he said in a semblance of his normal sardonic tones, 'If I hadn't called a halt I'd have taken you here and now on the front seat of the car within yards of your father's hotel, just like any woman of the street. Is that what you wanted?'

She was silent. Shame flooded through her. She had behaved like a wanton; she couldn't deny the charge.

'It's what I wanted,' Leon said harshly. 'You go to my head, Nita. I want to possess you as I've never wanted to possess a woman before.'

'So what stopped you?'

He paused deliberately. 'Perhaps I couldn't bear the thought of the recriminations afterwards.'

'Who says there would have been any?'

'Wouldn't there?' he asked. 'Your body I know I have. But your mind? Are you quite sure?'

She put her hand up to brush away a strand of hair that clung to her damp forehead. 'I'm not sure about anything at the moment.'

His hand went to the ignition and the car sprang into instant life. It took only seconds to reach the Hotel Cristobal where the night porter came hurrying down the steps to open the car door for her.

Nita turned to Leon. Conventional thanks for a pleasant evening seemed out of place in the light of what had just happened.

'I don't know what to say.'

'Don't say anything.' His eyes were enigmatic. 'But perhaps you'll do a little hard thinking about what you really want before we meet again.'

She got out and slammed the door behind her. And then, with a squeal of tires, he was gone.

# CHAPTER SEVEN

NITA slept badly that night. In her dreams Leon's dark figure pursued her endlessly down long, narrow corridors in a house that she had never visited before. His face was an implacable mask that held no sympathy for her. 'I want you!' he shouted after her as she fled from him. The words echoed all around her, mocking, taunting her until she put her hands up to her ears in an effort to blot them out.

'I want you, Nita.' She could still hear his voice behind her. It was coming closer. She tried to run faster, desperate to get away from him, but her feet were like lumps of lead and they wouldn't obey her. She opened her mouth to scream, but no sound came out. He was just behind her now. He was going to catch her and she didn't want him to. She mustn't give in; she must struggle. But she couldn't.

She woke with a jerk, her body damp with perspiration. The sheets were tossed about in wild disorder, testifying to the sort of night that she had had. She sat up weakly and pushed her hair away from her face with a hand that trembled slightly. On the table beside her bed the picture of the Aztec god mocked her. He had Leon's face. She stretched out a hand and turned him firmly to the wall. Damn the man! She punched her pillow viciously and wished it was Leon Calveto's head.

She wouldn't think about last night, she told herself. She went into the small bathroom that adjoined her bedroom and turned on the shower. But, as she stood motionless under its cool, refreshing spray, her mind rioted with a kaleidoscope of images that refused to be pushed away.

The pyramids bathed in that unearthly light and herself watching them, clutching Leon's jacket to her like a talisman; Maria and Emilio, their faces registering happiness and pleasure at the spectacle; the bright lights and conversation afterwards at the restaurant; the dimness of the car as Leon had driven her home. And then the memory of his touch, inviting, urging a response that she had been incapable of denying him.

'Your body I know I have,' he had told her. And it was true. Nita soaped herself vigorously as if the action could wash away her awareness of the fact. The effect he had on her was like a flame to dry tinder. In his arms she forgot everything. Pride, self-respect, reputation; none of them mattered in the least when Leon kissed her.

But kissing wasn't enough. She wanted it all. She wanted to feel the thrust of his body against hers as he showed her what physical love was all about. And he would be an expert tutor—she had no doubt of that. Would he be surprised, she wondered, to discover exactly how inexperienced she was?

What was she thinking of? He wasn't going to find out, Nita told herself as she stepped out of the shower and towelled herself briskly dry. When she gave herself to a man she wanted more than Leon Calveto was prepared to offer—a short-term affair leading nowhere.

That was all he had in mind. He wanted her, yes. And he wanted everything—not just her body, but her mind as well. And her heart too, if she was fool enough to show him that she had one to give. He would take the lot. But only until he tired of her. And then he would move on, she had no illusions about that; on to another lover. Or to marriage with one of his carefully chosen short list of suitable brides. He wouldn't be faithful to her either, thought Nita cynically.

She dressed and brushed her hair and applied her make-up more carefully than usual in an effort to conceal the ravages of last night. But she was only partially successful. Diego Lopez was a keen observer.

'You've got shadows under your eyes,' he told her bluntly, studying her across the breakfast table. 'Is something wrong?'

She wished she could have told him, poured out all her doubts and fears then and there. But he couldn't do anything to help. No one could. It was something that she would have to sort out for herself. There was no point worrying him unnecessarily.

She laughed convincingly. 'Nothing that a few early nights won't cure. I didn't get back until late.'

'A good evening?'

'Lovely. I must take you out to Teotihuacan some time. It's worth it.' She launched into a long description of the Sound and Light show and told him about Emilio and Maria. She thought her voice sounded strained and over-bright, but her father didn't appear to notice anything amiss. She must be a better actress than she thought she was.

'How was your evening?' she asked when she had run out of things to say on her own account.

'Hm? What?' Diego's mind seemed to be elsewhere.

'You're woolgathering!' she accused him. 'I don't believe you've heard a word I was saying!'

'I'm sorry, I was thinking about——'

'Business, I suppose. I knew it was a bad idea for you

to spend last night with your lawyer. I should have stayed and insisted that he left at a reasonable time.'

Diego Lopez gave a shout of laughter. 'I'd like to have seen you ordering old Fernando off the premises! He isn't used to liberated women. *His* daughters couldn't say "bo" to a goose.' He paused, then admitted, 'We did get through a fair amount of business. But it didn't take very long to sort out, as it happened.'

'He really shouldn't be bothering you with that sort of thing just now,' Nita scolded. 'What do you have a deputy for?'

'To make heavy weather of things that I used to do with one hand tied behind my back,' he grumbled. 'Oh, José's all right and he's as honest as they come. But he's a plodder and he lacks flair.'

'Not a whiz-kid like you, you mean.'

Diego laughed. 'Like I was once. I ate up the competition for breakfast! Whereas José lets everyone run rings round him while he works out his strategy.' He sighed. 'Oh, well, it won't be for much longer.'

'What won't be? You mean you're going to take over again?'

'No.' He hesitated, then told her, 'Nita, I've faced facts all my life, and I'm not going to start dodging issues now. These last few years I've been conning myself. I told myself I was as good as I ever was, that I'd go on in harness until I was ninety. I was a fool. I wouldn't let up.' He shrugged. 'And look what happened! I worked myself into a heart attack. And now——'

'And now what?' Nita was suddenly scared. 'Papa? You are all right, aren't you? Have you been keeping something from me? Did the doctor say something to you about——'

'Calm down!' he smiled. 'I'm not at death's door or anything like it. The doctor reckons I'll live to plague him for a good many years yet. If I take good care of myself, that is.'

'But?' she prompted him. 'There is a but, isn't there?'

'But there's a big difference between taking care of oneself and trying to run a multi-million-dollar operation the way that I've always run it. I never thought anyone could do things as well as I could. I never delegated. The pressure never let up. It needs a younger man, a fitter man, someone who can take stress and hard work in his stride and not let it get him down.'

'So?' Nita asked. 'What have you decided?'

'I'm selling out. I made my mind up a couple of weeks ago and the lawyers have been working it all out ever since. It can't be done in a hurry, that sort of thing.' He chuckled. 'And believe me, I've driven a fairly hard bargain!'

'I'm sure of that,' she smiled.

'The deal's all set up and there'll be an official handing over of power and signing of documents in a few days' time. I think it's for the best.'

'I'm sure it is,' she said firmly. 'You've given it the major part of your life. That's more than enough.'

'It's been my life, the business. At the cost of other things, I'm afraid. I realise that now.' He looked directly at her. 'You must have resented that in the past, Nita. I want to explain——'

'There's no need.'

'There's every need. I want you to understand the way it was, if you can. All those years ago when I started work first, I was determined to make money. I wanted to prove that I had it in me to get somewhere in life. I wanted to be a somebody. Nothing else mattered.

I went to work in America and I met your mother there. I was doing well by then, well enough to support a wife and family, so we married and I went from strength to strength.'

'And then?'

'It should have been enough to come home in triumph. Local boy makes good. Rags to riches.' He laughed. 'It's strange how one's never satisfied.'

Nita remembered Leon saying the same thing the previous night. But his goals weren't the same that her father had had.

Diego shifted uncomfortably in his chair as if he found it difficult to voice his next statement. 'I was obsessed with the idea of having an empire that I could hand on some day to my son, when the time came for me to bow out.' He laughed bitterly. 'So much for making plans! We had you, Nita, and then the doctor said there could be no more children. Your mother was disappointed—she would have liked a large family—but she accepted it.' He looked down. 'I—I found it harder to live with.'

An only daughter when he would have preferred an only son. 'Poor Papa,' Nita said softly.

'You can understand that? I didn't think you would. It wasn't that I didn't love you, Nita—just that I was disappointed that you weren't a boy.'

And girls rarely headed business empires in male-dominated Mexico, even in the second half of the twentieth century. It was a fact of life.

'So you buried yourself in work to forget?'

'What else was there to do? Besides, it was a habit by then, the only constant thing in life that didn't let me down or die. After your mother's death I think work was the only thing that kept me sane.' His eyes clouded.

'You know, everyone urged me to marry again. But I loved her too much to put anyone in her place.'

Nita stretched out a hand to him in sympathy. 'I'm glad you didn't.' As a child she had had fantasies about being part of a family, with brothers and sisters and two parents. But reality had never intruded on the dream, never shown her the disadvantages. There could have been any number. It would have been a difficult adjustment for her to make, she realised now.

Diego went on, picking his words with care. 'I neglected you shamefully when you were small. But, as you grew up, I saw the need to plan for your future. I thought you would marry some day, find a young man who could be groomed to take over the business——'

'And then you took one step further and decided that you'd select my future husband yourself because you didn't think I was capable of choosing correctly if you left me to my own devices.'

'Well, you weren't,' her father blustered. 'Antonio Diaz was a wastrel—admit it, Nita. He was interested in money, all right, but spending it, not making it. He'd have ruined the business inside six months if he'd ever taken over.'

'Probably. And I'd have discovered that for myself if I'd been allowed to. But instead, you suddenly played the heavy father, forbidding me to see him, announcing that you had someone else in mind for me.'

'What else could I have done?' he sighed.

'You could have used a little sense and tact in handling me instead of flying into a rage the way you did.'

'I was perfectly reasonable——'

'Oh, Papa, you weren't! You know you weren't——'

They glared furiously at each other across the table. Then Nita caught sight of their reflections in the mirror over the mantelshelf and saw the funny side of the argument. Two pairs of indignant brown eyes, two fiercely jutting chins, two scowls—identical in every respect. She began to laugh.

'I don't see anything funny,' said her father crossly.

'I do,' she said. 'What a picture we make, squabbling over something that doesn't matter now anyway. Climb down, Papa, and I will too. I really don't want another fight with you.'

Her father grunted, 'You'd try the patience of a saint!'

'Look who's talking! So would you.'

'Your mother used to tell me that,' he admitted grudgingly.

'And she loved you in spite of it—or because of it.' Nita looked at him with affection. 'And so do I. You know that, don't you?'

'I drove you away. I can't forgive myself for that.'

'It wasn't just your fault. It takes two to make a quarrel,' she told him earnestly. 'But that's in the past now, thank goodness. And we've still got the future, haven't we? And we're closer now as a result of all the misunderstandings. So at least one good thing came out of it all.'

'Yes,' he conceded. 'I just wish you would——'

But Nita didn't discover what it was that he wanted her to do. The telephone shrilled through the apartment just at that moment and Josefina entered the room to announce, 'Señor Guerrero on the line for you, *señor*. He says, can you spare him a moment?'

'José in a flap again! I'd better talk to him—I know what it will be about.' Diego Lopez got to his feet.

'So do I. Business,' Nita said ruefully. But she smiled as she told him, 'Don't overdo it, will you?'

'Don't worry.'

He went out of the room and Nita was left to her thoughts. She couldn't help feeling relieved that her father had made his decision of his own free will rather than at a doctor's urging. It was the best thing for him and he had the sense to see it for himself. Not that adjusting to retirement after all these years of frantic activity was going to be easy for him or those around him, she surmised. Except for golf, which he had taken up purely because of the opportunities it had given him to further his business contacts in a social atmosphere, Diego had no hobbies as far as she knew.

She would get him interested in something, she vowed. She would manage it somehow. It occurred to her that Diego hadn't told her the name of the company that he had sold out to. Not that it or its owner would mean a great deal to her, she supposed. She knew a lot of his business associates by name and had met some of them socially since her return home. But she couldn't say that she was on intimate terms with any of them.

Except Leon. The name suddenly flashed through her mind. A younger, fitter man, her father had said. That certainly described Leon. And Diego had made it all too clear what a high opinion he had of him. He had told her himself that he thought Leon would go far, given time and opportunity. Had he decided that he was a worthy successor?

Nita frowned as she poured herself another cup of coffee and sat sipping it reflectively. Something rang a bell on the fringes of her subconscious—something somebody had said last night. She had thought at the time that she would pursue the subject with Leon when they were alone together, but other things had assumed a great deal more prominence than idle questions, and she had pushed it to the back of her mind.

It was something that Maria had said. She had spoken about Leon's latest business deal when she had been teasing him about the need for fresh worlds to conquer. What was it she had said? Something about him acquiring a hotel chain. Nita had wondered idly about it, thinking of telling her father the news about one of his competitors, if he didn't know it already. She had never dreamt that it might be Diego's own empire that was up for sale.

It had to be Leon who had bought her father out. There couldn't be two hotel chains on the market at the same time. It would be too much of a coincidence. Why hadn't he said anything to her? Why hadn't her father said anything, for that matter?

She got up and went in search of Diego to question him further, only to hear from Josefina that he had taken the lift down to the main body of the hotel. He had wanted to talk to somebody urgently.

'I was just coming to find you, *señorita*, as it happens. He left this package of papers in my hand as he went. He wanted you to deliver them by hand to Señor Calveto at his office. He waited up last night, thinking that Señor Calveto might come back with you, but in the end he gave up and went to bed.' Josefina's wrinkled face held a knowing look. 'I could have told him he was wasting his time. A man like Señor Calveto makes the most of his time when he's out with a pretty girl!'

You could say that again, Nita thought wryly. 'You're incorrigible, Josefina,' she scolded the housekeeper, but with affection in her tone nevertheless. 'You'd matchmake for Dracula's mother, if you had the chance!'

'When you get to my age, *señorita*, the only romances that come your way are those of other people. Not that I'm complaining—I've had my share of admirers in my time.'

'I'm sure you have.' Nita took the bulky envelope reluctantly. She supposed it was urgent or her father wouldn't have asked her to do the errand for him. And presumably it was confidential too, or he would have sent it by one of the hotel staff. 'Thank you, Josefina, I'll see that Señor Calveto gets this safely.'

The last thing in the world that she wanted when she got up this morning was to confront Leon as soon as this; now it looked as if she hadn't much choice in the matter. She stood hesitating for a moment and then went to fetch a light jacket and her car keys. There was one thing about it—at least she would be able to establish whether Leon had bought the Lopez hotel group.

She had never visited his offices. There had been no reason for her to do so. But the address was on the envelope and she knew where it was, ten minutes' drive away along the road that led eventually to the University City and the Olympic Stadium. Traffic was light for once and it wasn't long before Nita was manoeuvring her way into a parking space beside a huge modern office block.

There was a commissionaire on duty in the vast marble entrance hall and he directed her to the lift after she had explained her business to him. She wanted the fourteenth floor, he told her. Señor Calveto's offices were on the right as she got out. He would ring ahead of her to make sure that she was expected.

Mercedes was waiting for her when the lift doors opened.

'Señorita Lopez.' Her greeting was cool. She held out her hand for the package. 'You needn't have come all the way up here, I could have collected that from downstairs.'

That put her firmly in her place, Nita thought. Messenger girl, third class. She didn't like that. She smiled sweetly at the other girl. 'Packages have a habit of getting lost that way. And this one is confidential, so I thought I'd better deliver it personally.'

'Well, now you have. Thank you.' The last words were bitten off as a definite afterthought.

'Personally to Señor Calveto,' Nita stressed.

'There's no need to——'

Nita knew that. But sheer cussedness on her part made her persist. 'There's every need. That's his name, not yours, on the envelope.'

'Leon's out at the moment.'

'Then I'll wait until he gets back.'

'That may be some time.'

'It doesn't matter. I haven't anything else planned for this morning.'

She thought that Mercedes was going to argue further, but evidently the other girl registered the firmness in her tone. The slender shoulders lifted in the suspicion of a shrug. 'Please yourself,' she said abruptly, then turned on her heel.

Nita followed the tiny figure, clad in a black dress that hugged every curve and showed off her impossibly slim waist, down the corridor and through an open door into what was obviously her office. A desk with an electric typewriter and attendant paraphernalia stood in one corner and a vast row of filing cabinets lined the whole of one wall. In the middle of another wall was a door, presumably leading to Leon's office, and Nita made for it.

'Leon doesn't like people being in his office without him there.' Mercedes' voice halted her in mid-stride. The other girl indicated a corner where a few easy chairs grouped round an arrangement of tropical plants were clearly placed for the reception of visitors. 'You'd better sit there.'

She wasn't imagining the unpleasantness in Mercedes' tone. It would be clear enough to anyone. Nita had no intention of being intimidated by her.

'Tell me,' she said coolly, as she watched the other girl move across to her desk and prepare to resume work, 'are you as rude as this to all Señor Calveto's clients, or is it just that you're singling me out for special attention for some reason or other?'

'What do you think?'

'I think you're insolent.'

'Pardon me for breathing! Complain to Leon when he gets back if it'll make you feel any better.'

'Aren't you scared that I might just do that?' asked Nita coolly.

Mercedes laughed. 'It won't get you very far. Leon won't dismiss me—not on your say-so or anyone else's. I'm too useful to him—both inside the office and outside. And very accommodating.' The jet dark eyes were malicious. 'How many women would take a back seat while he had a fling with another girl?'

'Is that what you call it?'

'Of course.' The other girl's glance swept over her, coolly assessing what charms she might hold for a man, visibly confident of her own superiority in that line. 'You're quite attractive, enough to take any man's eye—for a while at least. But you haven't got what it takes to hold a man like Leon.'

'No?'

'No.'

'And you have, I suppose?' Nita challenged.

'Yes. We had a good thing going before you arrived on the scene. He strayed, of course, from time to time. But men do. It's to be expected. I've always taken him back, and I will this time.'

'You're very tolerant,' observed Nita.

Mercedes shrugged carelessly. 'With Leon a girl has to be prepared to give a little. I don't particularly like seeing him paying court to another woman under my very eyes, but I make the best of it.'

If she did the mask slipped at times. Nita remembered the fury in Mercedes' face as she had upbraided Leon for attending Elena's engagement party without telling her he was going to be there, and for dancing the night away at the same party with Nita herself. A fury that had been matched by Leon's reaction to it. 'Mercedes doesn't matter,' he had told her then. But perhaps she did.

'Maybe one day Leon won't come back to you,' she suggested quietly.

'Is that what you're hoping?' The other girl gave an amused smile. 'You poor fool! You weren't beginning to dream of wedding bells, were you, by any chance? If you were thinking along those lines you should have worked a bit faster. Although I doubt if even the Lopez hotel empire would be worth such a sacrifice from Leon's point of view. He was prepared to go to quite a few lengths to keep you and your father sweet, but I don't think he'd have taken you to the altar. After all, you're only a night-club singer.'

'Keep me and my father sweet?' Nita frowned. 'What are you getting at? I don't understand.'

'Don't you? You surprise me. I didn't think you were stupid.'

'Perhaps I am. Spell it out to me.' She was suddenly tense.

'It's simple enough,' Mercedes told her. 'Leon's been wanting to get his hands on your father's hotels for some time now. He's made various offers over the years, but your father got as far as the talking stage and then backed off for a variety of reasons. Leon did everything he could to try to persuade him, but it never seemed enough. He wasn't ready to retire yet, he said. Things could have gone on like that for another twenty years or so. Then your father had this heart attack.'

'And Leon saw his way clear at last.'

'Practically. But there was a small cloud on the horizon.' Mercedes gave her a spiteful look. 'You.'

'But what had I to do with it all?'

'Quite a lot. Leon knew that your father wasn't easy in his mind about what happened to you. You walked out three years ago and he hadn't seen you since. But blood's thicker than water, and more so when you were all he had of a family. He was sick and he wanted you. So Leon volunteered to find you and bring you back home—anything to make the old man happy and win his approval. He was taking a risk, of course. For all he knew you might have married in the interim and provided Diego Lopez with a son-in-law worthy to inherit the empire.' Mercedes gave Nita a contemptuous look. 'It didn't seem likely on past form, but you never know—accidents happen.'

Nita ignored the slur. 'So?' she asked sharply.

'So it all went according to plan. He found you,

brought you home and was all set to get his reward. But
he couldn't be sure of anything for a while. You were
back on the scene and you might have influenced your
father in another direction or urged him not to sell at
all, if he'd consulted you about it. You might even have
taken it into your head to get engaged to one of those
chinless wonders who made up to you when you started
to do the social rounds. You might have wanted the
business for him, if you had. So——'

'So Leon took an interest in me himself and cut out
any possible rivals,' Nita muttered, half to herself, as
the realisation dawned on her.

'Got it in one! So long as he kept you sweet and
unaware of what was going on, he was laughing. You're
learning at last,' sneered Mercedes. 'He didn't have to
work very hard, did he? He never does with women. I
think it amused him how easily you succumbed once he
turned on the pressure a little. And Diego was delighted
that the two of you were getting on so well. Perhaps he
was thinking in terms of marriage bells too.'

In a daze Nita took in all the implications. It didn't
occur to her to question them; it was all so perfectly
plausible it had to be true. Mechanically she moved to a
chair and sat down. She felt numb.

'Have I shattered all your illusions?' The other girl
sounded pleased with herself. She must be satisfied to
have scored such a direct hit. 'I'm sorry if you thought
that Leon was such a lily-white character, pursuing you
with no ulterior motives.'

Oh, Nita had been aware of ulterior motives on his
part. But, naïvely, she had thought he was only out to
take advantage of her body, not that he had any farther-
reaching intentions. What a fool she had been!

She didn't want to see Leon now. The way she was feeling, she didn't want to see him ever again. She needed time to think. She had better leave now, before he got back.

'I won't stay to see Leon,' she said.

Mercedes was almost preening herself. 'Somehow I didn't think you would.' She indicated the package that Nita was still clutching to her. 'I'll take that, shall I?'

'Yes. Yes, you'd better.' Nita got to her feet and prepared to hand it over. Then she heard footsteps in the corridor and intuition told her that she had left it too late to make her getaway.

'Nita! I thought I recognised your car parked outside.'

She could have sworn Leon sounded pleased to see her. 'Hello,' she said briefly. She didn't look at him. 'I only came to deliver something to you from my father—he seemed to think it was urgent. I'll be on my way now.'

She could feel his eyes on her, willing her to look up at him as she put the package down on the desk in front of her. Instead she stared resolutely at the floor. She took two steps in the direction of the doorway and a pair of highly polished leather shoes came into her line of vision. They were blocking her path.

She tried to sidestep him, but he stopped her by the simple expedient of grasping her firmly by the arms. She had to look up then, one swift glance at his face. She could read nothing in his expression beyond the fact that it didn't suit him to let her leave yet.

'If there's any reply——' she began haltingly.

'If there's any reply you can take it with you when you go. Which won't be for a while yet.' He studied her keenly. 'Has Mercedes offered you a cup of coffee?' he asked her. 'You look as if you could use one.'

'I'm fine,' she lied. 'I don't need anything.'

'Good.' He didn't sound as if he believed her, but he

wasn't going to waste time arguing. 'Then we'll continue this discussion in my office.'

'I've nothing to discuss with you!'

'Well, I've plenty to say to you.' He ignored her instinctive movement of protest and pulled her with him towards the door that led to his room. Behind them Nita was aware of Mercedes' disapproving face. 'No calls, Mercedes.'

'But——'

'I said no calls. No interruptions at all. Under any circumstances.'

He opened the door with a powerful thrust of his shoulder and bundled Nita into the other office. The door banged shut behind them.

'You don't have to manhandle me to make sure that I do what you want!' snapped Nita.

'Don't I?' But he released her nonetheless and she retreated to stand a few paces from him, rubbing her bruised flesh. 'I could have used other means, but I didn't want to embarrass you in front of my secretary.'

'I didn't realise you were capable of showing so much consideration for my feelings!'

'No?' A dark brow rose sardonically. 'Why else do you think that I let you escape so easily last night, then?'

'I can't imagine.'

'Can't you?'

Nita averted her face. 'I don't want to talk about last night.'

'Is that why you're treating me like a leper this morning?' He gave an impatient sigh. 'For God's sake, Nita, look at me!'

Reluctantly she turned back towards him. She knew that if she didn't, he was quite capable of using force to ensure her obedience. 'Well?' she said, with an assumption of coolness. 'What is it you have to say? Whatever it is, I'll tell you now that I'm not interested in hearing it. I've heard quite enough lies from you already.' She laughed bitterly. 'And swallowed them. But fortunately my eyes are open at last.'

He could match her for cool control. 'What exactly do you mean by that?' he asked levelly.

'Can't you guess?'

'Suppose you tell me.' He moved towards the heavy mahogany desk that dominated the room and, stripping off his jacket, tossed it carelessly on to the chair that stood beside it, before turning to her again. 'I'm not in the mood for riddles of any kind this morning.'

He didn't look in the mood for anything at all, thought Nita as she studied his face in the strong light from the window. There was a grey tinge to his face and he looked tired to the bone. 'You look awful,' she told him.

'After I left you I sought a little consolation from the whisky bottle. It helped at the time, but this morning it doesn't seem such a good idea.' He ran a careless hand through his hair, ruffling its casual tidiness even more. 'It'll pass.' He glanced over at her, still standing by the door, as if poised for flight. 'Well?' he asked her. 'What am I supposed to have done?'

'You mean you've no idea?'

'Should I have? Unless it's the fact that I didn't make love to you last night——'

'I'm glad you didn't,' she told him vehemently.

'You could have fooled me.' She didn't like the look on his face. 'Then what?'

'My father told me he's selling the business.'

'That's right.' Even now he wasn't giving anything away.

'To you,' she continued. She didn't say that her father hadn't told her that.

'Yes.'

'Is that all you have to say?'

Leon shrugged. 'You're annoyed that nobody told you? Your father didn't think you'd be particularly interested. It's all been confidential up until now, anyway. You'd have heard eventually.'

'When it was too late to do anything about it!'

'It's too late now,' he said sharply. 'Not that it's any concern of yours. The deal is between myself and your father.'

'And you made darn sure that I didn't interfere, didn't you?' she flared. 'Tell me, are you proud of the way you went about the deal? First you con my father into believing that you really care about him—visits to his sick bed and then a special trip to fetch his erring daughter home. And then you work the same trick on me, making me believe you were really interested in what I had to offer you, that you enjoyed being with me——'

'I did,' he said tautly.

'Oh, that was one of the spin-offs, wasn't it? You'd have let me offer myself to you on a plate if I'd been fool enough! You wouldn't have said no. But you were scared of how it might rebound on you if you made love to me and then I changed my mind and confessed all to Papa. That was what you meant last night when you talked about recriminations, wasn't it?'

'You're talking rubbish,' he said.

'I don't think so!'

'My feelings for you come in a different category——'

'I can imagine! You reserve your finer emotions for my father's hotel chain, don't you? I'm just a fanciable body that you want to possess and that you can forget over a bottle of whisky!'

There was a ring of white around his mouth that told of temper kept firmly in check, but with an effort. 'I think you'd better go,' he said, and turned away to look out of the window.

Nita was strangely disappointed that he made no further effort to justify his actions to her. 'You realise that if I tell my father everything, he'll despise you as much as I do?'

Leon reacted to that, swinging round on her with an abruptness that scared her. 'You'll do nothing of the sort. Do you hear me?'

'Scared your precious deal might fall through after all?' she taunted him.

'If it does, think what it will mean to your father, rather than what it will mean to me,' he said. 'The worry, the pressure of finding another buyer, the inevitable fall in the share prices when it's generally known that the deal has collapsed. There'll be plenty of speculation that I was the one who pulled out at the last moment, not him, you know. And until it's allayed and a new buyer comes forward, who's going to fret and worry? Think about it, Nita, and think carefully, before you say anything at all.'

'You bastard!' she breathed.

He gave a mirthless smile. 'Think about it, Nita.'

For a moment she stood looking at him. 'I think I hate you,' she said. And then, without another word, she turned and left the room.

Mercedes wasn't in the outer office; perhaps she had been called away. Nita was glad she had gone. She went out and along the corridor to the lift without meeting anyone and got in it quickly when it came. Mercifully it was empty. As it carried her down to the ground floor again, she was conscious of tears trickling down her cheeks and, try as she could, she couldn't check them.

'I hate you,' she had said to Leon Calveto. But, to herself, she admitted the real truth. She loved him.


## CHAPTER EIGHT

THE signing ceremony was held a week later in the white and gold splendour of the Hotel Cristobal ballroom. It had been decided to make quite an event of the hand-over, with the press and leading members of the business community present, and the huge room was filled to capacity with friends, associates, and rivals, all eager to witness the completion of one of the biggest deals that had taken place in recent times.

If Diego Lopez was having last-minute regrets at handing over the reins of power, they didn't show. He circulated, chatting happily to everyone, apparently without a care in the world. Nita, who had stayed by his side in the initial stages, felt confident enough to leave him and make her own circuit of the room.

She talked to her father's deputy, José Guerrero, a quiet, shy man, who had a genius for figures and balance sheets, but little desire for corporate power. He had worked happily with her father for over ten years and had ably shouldered the burden of the decision-making process when Diego Lopez had been taken ill. But he had done so reluctantly, and he was clearly delighted to be stepping back from the limelight again.

He had nothing but good to say of his replacement in the hot seat.

'Just the sort of young man we need. A worthy successor to your father, I think. There couldn't have been a better choice. Everyone is absolutely delighted,' he told Nita enthusiastically.

She gave a noncommittal smile and moved on. But it was impossible to escape. The same sort of praise echoed in her ears time and again as she went from group to group. It seemed that her father had achieved the impossible and found as his successor a man who was universally approved.

Nita smiled and nodded in response until her face felt as if it was cracking in half with the effort of it all. She sought a brief respite and took refuge from the throng by one of the long open windows at the far end of the room where the heavy velvet drapes lifted slightly in the breeze from outside.

She closed her eyes for a moment in an attempt to blot out the glare coming from the lighted chandeliers that blazed down from the ceiling and the smoky atmosphere, caused by innumerable Havana cigars. She wondered if Leon had arrived yet; she hadn't seen his tall figure anywhere in the throng. Not that she wanted to, of course. She didn't care if she never saw him again. In fact, she would rather it was that way.

'Wishing you were somewhere else?' Almost as if her thoughts had conjured up his presence, his low-timbred voice sounded at her side.

Nita's eyes flew open. 'Yes,' she said deliberately. 'I got rather tired of hearing people sing your praises.'

Leon cast a cynical glance at the assembled crowd. 'I shouldn't take them too seriously. They'd be baying for my blood with equal fervour if it suited their purposes.'

'I wish they were!'

'Still nursing a grievance, Nita?' His tone was harsh.

'That's a mild way of putting it.'

'Yet you chose not to say anything to your father in the end.'

'Don't tell me you've been having sleepless nights worrying about the possibility?'

'Not in the least.'

No, she was the one who had lain awake until the early hours of the morning, analysing and assessing every move he had made, every statement he had uttered, trying desperately to find excuses for his actions.

She hadn't succeeded. There were no excuses for him. However she looked at it, the evidence pointed to the same conclusion: that Leon was nothing more than a cold-blooded business machine, who calculated his opponents' strengths and weaknesses with deadly accuracy and then made the best use of them to serve his own ends.

Nita looked across to where Diego was standing with a group of friends, laughing with them at some shared joke. 'I couldn't do it to him,' she said, 'as you knew perfectly well. So you're still his blue-eyed boy. Satisfied?'

He shrugged. 'What do you think?'

'If you're not, you should be. Or are you so used to getting your own way in everything that nothing gives you any pleasure any more?'

'Not at all. I still get a kick out of winning.'

'And the richer the prize, the greater the satisfaction, I suppose?'

'I wouldn't say that. Money doesn't mean a great deal to me. I've made enough of the stuff for it not to matter.'

'So what does matter then? demanded Nita. 'Power?'

'Authority,' he corrected. 'The chance to alter things for the better.'

'A giant ego trip for you, in other words!'

He shrugged. 'You could say that. I wouldn't.'

'Of course you wouldn't. But then people rarely see the truth about themselves, do they?' Nita told him. 'Well, you'll have your work cut out if you think that you can improve on my father's business.'

'Commendable loyalty, Nita, but ill-founded, I'm afraid. There's always room for improvement, even in the best-run establishments—as your father would be the first to agree. All the time he's kept me waiting I've used to best advantage by planning what I'd do when the deal finally came off.'

'You never had any doubts about it, did you? Patience must be one of your few virtues,' she said tartly.

'I usually get what I want in the end,' Leon agreed. 'You might do well to remember that.'

'And the people around you are just pawns in the game.' She gave a bitter laugh. 'Don't worry, that's something that I'm in no danger of forgetting about you.'

His eyes narrowed. 'You mean that you're determined suddenly to think the worst of me, for some reason.'

'I despise you,' she said bitterly. 'And your business methods. Is that clear enough for you?'

'Nita, I——' He stretched out a hand to her.

'Don't touch me!'

In spite of herself her voice rose, and a couple of elderly businessmen, chatting together a few paces from them, looked round in some surprise. Obviously Diego Lopez' daughter wasn't expected to squabble in public with his chosen successor.

'We can't talk now,' Leon said impatiently.

'No.'

'But we will talk.'

'Not now or in the future. I'm not interested in what you have to say!'

'Damn you, you'll——'

'Oh, there you are.' Mercedes' cool voice broke in on the argument. 'I've been looking all over for you.'

The other girl was wearing red today, a flaming, vibrant red that enhanced her dark good looks and made Nita's pink linen dress seem as demure as a schoolgirl's in contrast. Mercedes' fingernails were a matching shade, Nita noted absently, as one beautifully manicured hand pawed Leon's sleeve to attract his attention.

'Sorry if I'm breaking anything up.' She smiled up at him, confident that she had not and completely ignoring Nita. 'But I've been sent to find you. Everything's about ready for you, if you feel like coming over. The press people are all organised, and Señor Lopez is waiting for you.'

'Sure.' Leon's interest switched with insulting swiftness from Nita to the matter closest to his heart. 'Let's go, shall we?'

The instruction seemed to be aimed at Mercedes rather than her, so Nita stood where she was, watching him wend his way through little knots of businessmen back towards the centre of the ballroom where an impressive marble-topped table stood ready for the signing session.

For all her words of defiance to him, Nita couldn't take her eyes off his figure as he strode across the room, Mercedes' tiny form struggling to keep up in his wake.

Mentally as well as physically he dwarfed every man in sight.

The transfer of power took a very short time—the principals' signatures on first one document and then its duplicate, and then those of the chief executives on both sides. Handshakes and a quick *abrazo* all round and the deed was done. Nita saw her father make signs towards the waiters who were standing ready with trays of champagne and they moved forward to serve everybody in order that they could toast success to the venture.

The press photographers moved in again. There were pictures of Diego and Leon shaking hands, bending forward to examine the document they had just signed, talking to each other animatedly. And then the lesser dignitaries had their turn. And her father was calling her forward to include her in some of the group photographs.

'You don't want me in on this,' she protested.

'Of course we do.' Diego's voice was insistent. 'There've been too many pictures of old fogeys—saving your presence, Leon. It's time there was a bit of glamour included!'

He held out his hand to her and Nita was forced to comply. Just to make him happy, she told herself, as she posed between him and Leon. She was acutely aware of the tall, powerful figure on the other side of her as she smiled dutifully into the cameras. She wondered if Leon could tell how her treacherous senses blazed into life when the photographers asked them to move closer together for one picture and she felt the firm pressure of his thigh against hers and the touch of his hand on her shoulder, steadying her to hold the position. At the first opportunity she moved hastily away. She didn't trust herself.

Someone pushed a glass of champagne into her hand and she drank mechanically to the new order of things.

'Long life and prosperity to you, Leon,' her father called, and the toast echoed round the room, to be followed by others.

Just like a wedding, Nita thought. And, no doubt, a good deal more to Leon's taste than that kind of ceremony would be. Another stronghold had fallen to him; another triumph had come his way. She could hardly bear to look at the satisfaction in his face. Across the crowded room his head swung round in her direction, as if he sensed her feelings. He raised his glass mockingly to her, then turned away to the small, flame-red figure by his side.

Nita slipped away. She couldn't take any more. When her father came back to the apartment more than an hour later, she told him that she had had a headache.

'Too much champagne, when I'm not used to it,' she explained and, mercifully, he looked no farther as a reason for her absence.

Over the next few days the popular press was full of news of the merger, covering the event lavishly.

'Thousands of dollars' worth of free publicity there,' Diego commented approvingly as he scanned the results in a magazine.

'Yes.' Nita looked at the photograph of Leon with her father and herself that had been printed there. She was amazed how carefree she looked. So the camera could lie occasionally.

The headline read, 'Calveto makes another killing.' The crude language of the concrete jungle summed it all up. The business world was, above all, a place where one fought for survival.

And Leon was a born survivor, a successful predator who would go from strength to strength. He looked the part, too, Nita thought, studying the glossy colour photograph. A perfectly tailored dark suit, teamed with an immaculately white shirt and a grey silk tie, gave an impression of cool authority. Hand-tooled shoes on his feet and a heavy gold watch on his wrist were discreet symbols of wealth. His hair was brushed ruthlessly back from his forehead, his chin jutted upwards in an aggressive line. He looked supremely confident of his ability to dominate the world around him. And that included her, she suspected, noting the possessive angle of his body against hers.

She hadn't seen him since the signing session. But it could only be a matter of time before she encountered him again. She couldn't bear it. She needed time to herself to think. She must at least try to get him out of her system. She wondered where to go—and whether her father would be upset if she announced plans to go off on her own for a week or so. She hesitated to broach the subject to him.

Deliverance came in a long-distance phone call from Maria. Nita had given the other girl her number, but had hardly expected to hear from her so soon.

'I've been wondering how you were getting on. Is everything going all right with you?' Nita asked.

'I'd like to say I'm fine, but I'm not,' groaned Maria.

'No? But what——'

'Morning sickness. I know it'll pass eventually, but at the moment it's driving me out of my mind,' Maria sighed. 'And I feel so tired! I've been moping rather. So Emilio came up with a marvellous idea—to cheer me up, you know. He realised how I took to you when we met the other week and he thought it would take my mind off my troubles if you were to come out here to visit us.'

'Maria, that's a——'

'Well, you did say you would visit us soon, didn't you? And you don't know how wonderful it would be just to see a new face around me. My mother-in-law lives just round the corner and she's been very nice— well, nice for her, that is. But it's not the same as someone young and sympathetic, if you know what I mean——'

'Perfectly.' Nita tried to stem the babble from the other end of the line. 'But are you sure you want to be bothered with a visitor? I——'

'Would I be asking you if I wasn't sure? Of course I want you to come and stay for as long as you can.'

'Well, if you promise faithfully that you'll tell me the minute that you've had enough of my company——'

'Then you will come?' Maria sounded delighted. 'That's the best news I've had all week!'

'I'm not a miracle worker, you know,' Nita warned. 'Don't expect all your problems to vanish the instant I cross the threshold.'

'Nonsense! It'll be a tonic just to see you,' Maria told her happily. 'And Emilio will be as pleased to have you here as I will. I think he's been a bit worried about me. He doesn't say very much, but he's been clucking round me like a mother hen these last few days.'

Nita promised to make her arrangements as swiftly as possible and said she would phone details of her flight as soon as she had it. When she finally rang off and went in search of her father to tell him about her intended trip, she felt as if a weight had been lifted from her. Maria's invitation couldn't have come at a better time.

'Of course, I won't go, if you'd rather I stayed here to look after you,' she said to Diego.

He snorted indignantly. 'Look after me indeed! You can stop treating me like an invalid. I'm practically my old self again now. I feel better than I've done for years.' He caught the sceptical look in her eye. 'Ask the doctor, if you don't believe me. Anyway, it's not as if you'll be at the end of the world. Merida's only a short flight away. So go and book your ticket with a clear conscience.'

Nita laughed and did as he said. The Yucatan Peninsula was always a popular tourist stop and flights were often booked days in advance, but she managed to get a seat on a plane in two days' time. That gave her sufficient breathing space to pack and organise those details of the running of the household that she had taken over by way of helping Josefina. And, with a bit of luck, it meant that she wouldn't see Leon before she left.

But luck wasn't with her. On the eve of her departure, as she was in the last stages of packing her cases, her father called out to her.

'Is something wrong, Papa?' He was standing by the phone, registering some impatience.

'I've been trying to get hold of Rivera for the last half hour,' he told her, looking impatiently at his watch. 'The manager's on duty at the moment and he should be available, but he's just not answering his phone.'

'He's probably been called away for something. He's bound to be somewhere in the hotel.'

'So I imagine. But I haven't time to track him down. I've got a car waiting.'

'Was it something urgent?' asked Nita. 'I could pop down to the hotel and look for him.'

Bernardo Rivera had run the Hotel Cristobal since its inception and Nita had known him since childhood. She didn't mind going in search of him and delivering a message, particularly if it set her father's mind at rest. He wasn't supposed to get agitated; it wasn't good for him.

'Would you, Nita?' Diego looked relieved. 'He was going to drop by tonight for a drink and a game of chess and perhaps a little chat about old times. But I'd forgotten, when I told him to come this evening, that I was already promised to the Alayas, and they live over on the other side of the city. I don't really want to go, but I've already cried off twice, and they'll be offended if I don't turn up.'

Nita laughed. 'Don't worry, I'll go and make your excuses to Señor Rivera. I expect he'll forgive you.'

'Yes, he'll understand. He's an obliging chap. Which is more than I can say for Felipe Alaya,' Diego added ruefully. 'Oh well, I'd better get off there.' Her father took up his coat and prepared to leave. 'You won't forget, will you?'

'I'll come down with you right this minute,' she assured him, following him to the lift.

In the lobby she saw her father stride off to the front entrance where a chauffeur-driven limousine was waiting for him. She smiled. He was looking better, she thought. There was a spring in his step and a jauntiness in the way that he carried his head. He was right; she could leave him with a clear conscience.

She strolled casually through the crowded foyer and made for the door labelled Hotel Manager at one side of the plush reception area. It was probably best to try the office first in case he had returned there while she and her father had been taking the lift down. If she drew a blank there, she could try the catering manager's office or the hotel accounts department. And, if all else failed, she could have him paged.

But it looked as if she had found her quarry at her first attempt. The office door was half open and she could hear the rustle of papers from inside. Relieved, she tapped gently and, with the ease born of long years of familiarity with all her father's staff, didn't wait to be told to enter, but walked straight in.

But the figure bending over some papers laid out on the battered desk that took up a good half of the floor space wasn't the short, plump form of Bernardo Rivera. It was Leon.

'I thought I gave strict instructions that I wasn't to be—' He turned his head and registered Nita's presence. He got to his feet. 'What are you doing here?'

He was dressed in usual style, but casually, in a light woollen sweater and dark cords that hugged his long legs. He looked strained, she thought, as if he had been working for long hours without a break in the aftermath of the take-over. If that was what business deals did to you, she was glad her father was out of it all at last.

'I was looking for Señor Rivera,' she told him.

'He's not here at the moment.'

'I can see that,' she said. Reaction made her voice shrill and she tried to pull herself together. Act normally, she told herself. Don't let him throw you. 'Do you know where he is? I've got a message for him from my father.'

'He'll be back shortly, I expect. You'd better come in and wait.'

'It's all right. I needn't——' She floundered. 'That is, I can——'

'Scared of being alone with me, Nita?' Leon mocked her.

'Of course not!'

The door had swung to behind her and she had the strangest feeling of being trapped. She was being ridiculous, she told herself. Leon was hardly likely to try something on here in his own manager's office of all places. She was getting paranoid about the man! All the same, there was something about the curiously intent way that he was studying her that made her distinctly uneasy.

'You must be working very hard,' she said with an attempt at brightness, looking past him towards a sheaf of papers which he had been studying when she had interrupted him.

He shrugged. 'I always work hard. I like to know as much about what's going on as my staff do.'

'Papa always says that—said that, I mean,' she corrected herself hastily. It was difficult to adjust to the fact that her father was no longer in control of all this. 'He never stopped for anything. He worked frantically hard.' She was conscious that she was talking slightly too fast out of nerves. 'I'm sorry if I've distracted you. Please do go on with whatever you were doing.'

'It can wait,' he said carelessly. 'I think that just now I prefer to be distracted.' He took a step towards her and it was an effort on her part not to start back in reaction. 'After all, it's nearly a week since I had the pleasure of your company. And you absented yourself pretty speedily then.'

That had been at the signing ceremony.

'Don't tell me you missed me? I'd have thought you were too taken up with Mercedes to notice that I wasn't there.'

'Were you jealous?' he taunted her. 'Was that why you left?'

'Not at all. I had a headache.'

'It came on rather suddenly, didn't it?' he drawled.

'Yes, it did, as a matter of fact.'

'Liar,' he said without heat. 'Admit it—you ran away.'

'I did nothing of the sort!'

His eyes narrowed. 'You did. And you're still intent on running, aren't you? Your father tells me you're going to stay with Maria and Emilio.'

'And what if I am?' she challenged him. 'I wasn't aware that I had to ask your permission!'

'It won't work, you know.'

'What won't work?'

'Dodging the issue. There's no point trying to run away from me, Nita. I'll catch up with you in the end.'

She forced a laugh. 'Is that why you think I'm going? To escape from you?'

'Isn't it?' His glance was shrewd.

'I'm going because I want to see Maria again. And because I've never been to the Yucatan and I've always wanted to. Satisfied?'

Leon shrugged. 'O.K. Have it your way, then, if it makes you feel any better. But bear in mind that absence makes the heart grow fonder.'

'Not in this case. I've every intention of forgetting your existence.'

'That would be a pity. Perhaps I'd better give you something to remember me by.'

Nita guessed his intention and moved back towards the door. But she hadn't a hope of escaping. His longer legs covered the distance between them in a couple of easy strides and one hand came out to draw her effortlessly to him while the other reached behind her to secure the door from unwelcome intruders.

'It appears that there's only one satisfactory way of communicating with you, Nita,' he said harshly. 'Let's try it, shall we? It might get us somewhere for a change.'

'I don't want you,' she claimed. 'I don't want you! Do you hear?'

'Who are you trying to convince, Nita?' he asked her, and, without waiting for an answer from her, took possession of her lips in a kiss that made her senses reel.

Her nerve ends splintered in a thousand pieces of delight and merged again in a wave of mingled passion and desire. Holding back was like trying to stem a floodtide. But she couldn't give in to him. He had used her quite coldbloodedly to obtain his own ends. And, despising him as she did, there was no way that she was going to meekly surrender to him. He doesn't care, her brain told her. He never will. Don't trust him.

'Respond, damn you!' His lips left hers briefly, impatiently, to mutter the words against her ear as he realised she was holding out on him. 'Give, Nita, give—I want you!'

And she wanted him, God knows. Her whole body ached with the effort of denying him. Leon pressed her still closer to him, moulding the soft curves of her body against the unyielding hardness of his, making her all too aware of the extent of his own arousal.

She would have to give in. She couldn't stand it any longer; she had no choice. There was a languid warmth creeping through her, drugging her, blurring her ability to think clearly about anything any more. She had done her best to resist him, but her best wasn't good enough.

There was a hammering in her head, a drumming

sound. For a split second Nita thought that the noise was the pounding of her own heartbeat. Then, as the sound continued, she was suddenly conscious that it had nothing to do with her. Someone was knocking at the office door.

Leon snapped back to sanity at almost the same instant, releasing her abruptly as if she had suddenly become red-hot.

'One moment!' he called.

Nita could see him fighting and winning the battle to control himself, although his voice, when he finally turned the catch and bade whoever it was outside to enter, had an unaccustomed roughness. The atmosphere in the room was electric; Nita could almost feel the charge in the air.

'I'm sorry.' The bewildered expression on Bernardo Rivera's face as to why he should be barred from his own office cleared and changed to a slightly knowing look when he realised that Nita was keeping his new boss company. 'I didn't realise you had someone with you. Señorita Lopez.' He inclined his head deferentially to Nita and she managed to find a smile for him.

'Señorita Lopez had a confidential message for me from her father,' Leon explained, and his expression dared his manager to challenge him.

'Of course.' Rivera's voice was bland, but there was speculation in his eyes.

'And I have a message for you as well, Señor Rivera.' Nita delivered it rapidly and then, all too conscious of her flushed face and swollen lips, which must bear clear evidence of Leon's kisses, she excused herself. 'I'm sure you must have a lot of things to dicsuss. I'll leave you together.'

There was nothing Leon could do to stop her,

although she could see by the ominous firming of his mouth that he wasn't best pleased with the situation. She slipped past him to the door, which the older man hastened to hold open for her.

'My regards to your father, *señorita*. If you could tell him that I'll be along to see him tomorrow night instead?'

'I'll do that, Señor Rivera.'

'You won't forget what I told you?' Leon spoke after her.

'To enjoy myself in Merida?' Nita deliberately chose to misunderstand him. 'No, of course not.' She paused in the doorway and managed a cool smile. 'Believe me, I can't wait to get away. It'll be so nice to have a little civilised company for a change!'

She left on that parting shot. No doubt it would give rise to even more speculation on Bernardo Rivera's part. But, if he was wise—and she knew he was—he would keep it to himself. As Nita made her way back to the penthouse she was lightheaded with relief at her escape.

Next day, on the plane to Merida, she relaxed and looked forward to the break. A week, maybe two weeks, in different surroundings and with different people and she would be a new person, she told herself confidently. She had been under a fair amount of strain, one way and another, in the last few weeks. Worry about her father had been succeeded by a different type of worry about Leon and his intentions. She hadn't really been thinking straight recently.

So she thought she was in love with Leon. So what? Three years ago she had imagined she was in love with Antonio Diaz. And now she found it hard to remember what he looked like and the pain that she had felt at the time had faded. And the same process would take place over her feelings for Leon, she vowed, determinedly ignoring the knowledge that Antonio had never brought her the awareness of her body and its needs that Leon had forced upon her. Antonio had made her conscious of love as a girlish emotion. Leon had demanded a woman's response from her.

There were other men in the world. She was sure that Maria knew any number of eligible bachelors and would be delighted to introduce her to them. Somewhere there had to be a man who wouldn't let her down and who could be trusted. Perhaps, in Merida, she might find him.

The airport was small compared to the one that she had left and it was swarming with people. Emilio was waiting to greet her and take her luggage.

'It's good to see you again,' he said with a friendly smile. 'We're both looking forward to having you stay for as long as you can. Who knows, you may decide never to go back to the big city?'

'Perhaps,' Nita laughed. That would certainly be one solution to her problems. 'How's Maria?'

'Feeling the heat a little today. She insisted on coming out to the airport with me, but I managed to persuade her to stay in the car with the air-conditioning unit switched on while I came to find you. The last thing I wanted was for her to faint in the middle of the arrivals hall!'

He opened the swing doors for her to go through, and Nita understood what he meant. She had left Mexico City on a hazy day with the temperature in the mid-sixties. Here it was more like ninety degrees and the sun blazed down from a sky so blue that it dazzled the eyes. Her forehead was wet with perspiration even in the short walk to the car, and she was grateful for the blast of cool air that hit her as she got inside and shut the door.

Maria was looking a bit pale, Nita noticed, but her welcome was as enthusiastic as that of her husband, and she brushed aside her visitor's sympathetic questions about her health. 'I'll be right as rain now that you've come,' she declared. 'I'm really looking forward to showing you everything. I've been planning all sorts of outings that we can take. I'm really going to enjoy myself!'

'So am I, if I don't melt away in this heat,' said Nita as she mopped her streaming brow.

'You'll get used to it, everyone does after a few days. Although it even catches us natives out occasionally. What you need is a cool drink and a rest. You'll feel fine then.'

The journey into town took little time and, enlivened as it was by running comments from her hosts, she was almost sorry when it ended.

Emilio gave her a brief history of the city. 'It was established in the sixteenth century by the son of one of Cortes' captains who had been given a royal grant from Spain to colonise the Yucatan. And it's still a colonial city in many ways. You can see the Spanish-Moorish look to the buildings with thick walls and flat roofs. And, of course, the colour-washed walls. We haven't any skyscrapers out here yet, thank goodness. Not that they won't come in time,' he told her gloomily.

'You'd think he hated progress, to hear him talk!' Maria rounded on her husband. 'And how many times have I heard you complain about the narrow streets that also date from colonial times? There's no way of parking outside some of the hotels in the centre of town, Nita. It would block the traffic entirely. So Emilio has to leave his mini-bus quite a distance away and go and fetch his groups of tourists on foot. You should hear him grumble about it!'

'Oh, well, I suppose it keeps me fit,' Emilio allowed, and Maria hooted unsympathetically.

'That's what you ought to use,' she said, pointing out a horse-drawn carriage that was proceeding in a leisurely fashion along the road that led to the main square. 'They go everywhere, and the tourists love them.'

'So long as they get a carriage with a few springs in it still. Last time I went in one I was bruised all over after an hour's drive, we bumped up and down so much.'

'I never heard a word about the discomfort when you used to take me out in one on Sunday afternoons before we were married.'

'Perhaps I had other things to think about.'

Maria gave him an arch look. 'That's love for you, Nita! It's a wonderful thing.'

'So they tell me.' Nita kept her tone light. 'Hey, what's that building over there on the other side of the square?'

Maria leaned forward to identify it as the Palacio Municipal and the moment passed.

Maria and Emilio's house was a large, comfortable building dating from the turn of the century. Spanish in tone, it was delightful, with cool, marbled floors and white walls. The windows had wrought-iron grilles to them and doors in the same pattern led off to the rear where there was a cool patio, fragrant with the scent of tropical flowers.

The two girls sat there to enjoy the ice-cold drinks that were served by a young maid whose dark features betrayed her Indian ancestry. Emilio excused himself, pleading business at the office that he had to attend to personally.

'Don't wear Nita out with your chatter,' he warned his wife as he left.

Maria giggled. 'Emilio always says that if I hadn't anyone to talk to, I'd talk to myself. And the awful thing is, he's probably right!'

Nita laughed. Maria's brand of bubbly happiness was just what she needed. She had been right to come here, she thought.

The other girl leaned forward in her chair. 'Now, tell me what's been happening in the Big Smoke,' she commanded. 'I want to hear it all—the latest fashions that you've seen in the boutiques, the scandals in high society, everything you can think of to tell me. We get a bit cut off here, being so far from anywhere.' She clapped a guilty hand to her mouth. 'Don't tell Emilio I said that, will you? He's a Yucateco first and a Mexican a long way second. He wouldn't live anywhere else. I'd love to be in Mexico City, but Emilio would never hear of it, so what's the use?'

'It's fine for a visit. But you'd soon be crying out for blue skies and hot sunshine if you were there all the time,' Nita told her.

'That's what Leon says.' Maria was off on another tack. 'How is he, by the way? I've tried to get hold of him any number of times since we've been back, but all I ever got from his home number was no answer, and when I tried his office I got some bitchy girl who kept telling me he was unavailable.'

'Mercedes,' Nita identified immediately. 'His secretary.'

'Oh, is that her name? Well, she was very rude to me.'

Maria frowned at the memory. 'I think she thought I was an ex-girl-friend of Leon's to be fended off. One can't blame her, I suppose.'

'I suppose not.' Nita's tone was carefully neutral.

'So tell me, how is he?'

'Fine. Busy doing what he enjoys most in the world—empire-building. I haven't seen a great deal of him lately.'

'That's a pity.' Maria gave her a shrewd look. 'I saw his picture in the paper. It was your father's hotel group that he took over, wasn't it?'

'Yes.'

Maria seemed inclined to pursue the subject, in spite of Nita's clear reluctance to discuss it. 'You know, when I saw the two of you together I hoped something was going to come of it.'

'Something did—mutual dislike,' Nita assured her.

'That I don't believe.'

'It's true,' Nita said tautly.

'Would it help to talk about it?'

Nita hesitated, then shook her head. 'No, Maria, it wouldn't. Thank you all the same.'

The other girl looked upset. 'If there's anything I can do, you will say, won't you?'

'Only one thing. Help me to forget that a man called Leon Calveto ever existed.'

# CHAPTER NINE

NITA suspected that Maria must have had a quiet word with her husband on the subject of her feelings for Leon, and she was grateful to them both for the tact that they displayed. In the days that followed his name was never mentioned and her new friends did all they could to keep her occupied, plunging her into a whirl of activity, clearly designed to give her barely time to draw breath, let alone brood.

It was a strategy that worked to a limited degree. Maria was a lively companion and Nita enjoyed seeing the town through her eyes and hearing her often irreverent comments about its inhabitants. Dutifully she took Nita to the usual tourist sights; the grim, fortress-like cathedral, the governor's palace, with its beautiful paintings, and the Museum of Archaeology, housed in one of the gracious, turn-of-the-century buildings that lined the Paseo de Montejo. But she obviously preferred showing off the things that gave her pleasure; the numerous shady gardens that were dotted all over Merida and the markets, a never-ending source of delight for her.

'Emilio swears that all his profits go straight into the pockets of the market traders,' she told Nita with an impish grin. 'But I do so enjoy poking about here, and it's awfully hard to go home without falling for something. There's always something new. Look over there.' She grabbed Nita's arm. 'Those brooches on that stall!'

Nita followed her gaze. Displayed on a piece of black velvet, the brightly jewelled objects seemed to her eye to be moving about. 'They're not alive, are they?'

'Of course they're alive. They catch beetles and the like and stick shiny stones on their backs. You're meant to wear them on your lapel.'

Nita watched in horrified fascination. 'Not for me. Suppose it crawled down your neck by mistake?'

'They can't. They're tethered by tiny chains attached to the brooch pin.'

'Rather you than me,' Nita shuddered. 'Anyway, I'm sure it's cruel.'

'I can see Emilio's face if I bought one,' Maria giggled. 'Well, perhaps not. What about something else to wear? One of those embroidered *huipiles*? That one with the red embroidery would look wonderful on you.' She dashed over to examine the dress more closely and Nita followed her, smiling at her enthusiasm and the stallholder's swift approach in anticipation of a sale.

In some ways Maria reminded her very much of Sandy, although her friend in Miami was a good deal younger. Both were impulsive and endlessly talkative. Both were generous to a fault and good-humoured. And, like Sandy, Maria had a zest for life and determination to wring the last drop of pleasure she could get out of it.

Of course it must be easy to be happy and carefree when you had all that Maria had—a lovely home, servants to look after it, money in the bank, a doting husband and now the prospect of achieving the one thing that had so far been denied her, a healthy child to complete the picture. Nita envied her from the bottom of her heart, however much she tried not to.

Possessions didn't matter. But what wouldn't she give

to have a marriage like Maria's, a teasing, laughing partnership full of genuine liking as well as love? Emilio had been Maria's first boy-friend.

'I made up my mind that I was going to marry him the day that I met him,' she confided to Nita on one occasion. 'I was only fifteen then. It was lucky that he felt the same way that I did and waited for me to grow up a little, or I don't know what I would have done.'

'You'd have got him in the end.'

'I expect so,' Maria agreed shamelessly. 'Even if I'd had to stick any number of daggers in the competition. I always think you can get anything you want if you set your mind to it and try hard enough.'

'Perhaps.'

It depended, of course, on what you wanted. And Nita was beginning to doubt whether any amount of concentrated effort would block out the memory of what Leon had been to her. What he still was. Try as she might to think about other things, there seemed to be reminders of him at every turn. A tall man with broad shoulders and just Leon's confident stride, who stopped her in her tracks in the middle of the square, until he turned his head and revealed a coarse-featured face, pitted with acne scars. A low-timbred voice, heard in a shop while she was waiting to be served. She had whipped round quickly, only to come face to face with a total stranger.

Her imagination hadn't played tricks on her like this when she had split up with Antonio. And she had loved him. Or had she? She was beginning to doubt it now. She had cried when he had disillusioned her; how she had cried! But, looking back, Nita thought now that a lot of her tears had been because of her own hurt pride, not for any other reason. There hadn't been this awful feeling of black despair, of deprivation..

At night Nita tossed and turned on the narrow guestroom bed and tried to come to terms with the situation. But she woke in the morning only to the knowledge that she had failed. She didn't know how much of her private anguish Maria and Emilio guessed at. Certainly she made every effort to behave in their company like an appreciative guest who was enjoying her stay enormously.

She caught Maria's eye on her occasionally in a thoughtful fashion, but the other girl said nothing. A couple of times Nita was tempted to take up her offer of a sympathetic ear for her problems, but she decided in the end that it wasn't fair to involve her. After all, Leon was a friend of many years' standing and she had only just got to know them. If Maria believed her story, it would mean divided loyalties for her. If she didn't, it would mean the end of their new friendship, and that was the last thing that Nita wanted.

So she threw herself more vigorously into trying to enjoy life. She could have spent an agreeable time wandering through the narrow streets, alone or in Maria's company. But there were other options open.

'Why not come out with me on a couple of trips?' Emilio offered. 'There's always a spare seat going on the bus, even if we're fully booked. That is, if you don't mind hugging the first-aid box to you. It usually sits on a little bucket seat at the back.'

'I'd love to. But if Maria——'

'Maria wouldn't come if you paid her. She'll stay at home and rest, just like the doctor ordered. She's been doing a little too much dashing around lately,' Emilio decreed.

'Tyrant!' Maria pulled a face, but complied willingly enough. 'Clambering about old ruins and the like isn't my idea of a good time,' she told Nita. 'I get hot and tired and very bored. And Emilio is so terribly thorough. I'm sure most of the other tour operators do a quick round of the points of interest and leave the tourists to it while they retire to the nearest place where they can get a cool drink and a rest. But not my husband!' She threw him an affectionate glance. 'He has to give a lecture on each individual stone.'

Emilio only grinned, taking her teasing in good part. 'Some people prefer it that way—and just be thankful they do. They go home and recommend me to their friends, and that's why business is booming.'

'Emilio's going to expand next season,' said Maria, proud of her husband's achievement. She chuckled, looking down at her still slender figure. 'I told him, I'm expanding this year and you can do it next.'

So, along with Emilio's paying customers, Nita marvelled at the ancient ruins of Uxmal and Chichen Itza, climbing to the top of pyramids just as high and splendid as those that she had seen at Teotihuacan. Only this time there was no tall striding figure by her side. At least the underground caves at Balancanche didn't bring back any memories—they were a new experience and one that Nita enjoyed.

'Aren't those masses of stalactites coming down from the roof of the cave fantastic?' she exclaimed in amazement to one of her fellow travellers, a stout German woman.

The woman only grunted and said with an anxious expression on her plain, broad face, 'I wonder I can get out in safety. Coming in, I stick to the sides.'

Nita sympathised. Some of the passages were a bit cramped. Thank goodness she'd never had a weight problem!

She told her father about the incident when she made one of her regular phone calls home to him, and he laughed. 'You sound as if you're having a good time out there.'

'Terrific!' she lied dutifully. 'One of these days I'll drag you out here for a holiday. It's beautiful, and every morning when I wake up the sun's shining—at least it has done so far.'

But Diego wasn't sold on the idea. 'Give me a good healthy smog any day of the week,' he told her. 'I'd be lost without it.'

She deliberately prolonged the conversation, hoping he might drop a stray remark about Leon, tormenting herself by wondering what he was doing. Had he been seen round the town with a new woman, or was Mercedes back in evidence? Her father didn't seem inclined to mention him and she was too conscious that her voice might betray her if she asked about Leon directly. Besides, how did one ask that sort of question? She led up to the subject by a side route.

'How's the business going under the new management?'

'Don't tell me you're actually interested?'

'Shouldn't I be?' she forced a laugh. 'Perhaps I'm developing new hobbies at last in my old age. After all, I'll be twenty-three next birthday.'

Diego chuckled knowingly. 'That's not the reason, is it? I understand perfectly well why you're asking, so don't try and pull the wool over my eyes.'

'You do?' she stammered. Was her love for Leon so transparent?

'It's good of you, Nita, to pretend that you care about the sort of things that I'm keen on, just because you think I like talking about it all, and I probably don't get many opportunities to discuss it now. But you don't have to picture me at home, pining for it all.'

'I don't?' she said, only relieved that he had picked the wrong reason for her query.

'As a matter of fact, now the pressure's off, I'm rather enjoying myself. I was in Cuernavaca last week, looking at a development for a block of holiday homes—and you know, I haven't had such a good time in ages. Of course, it was someone else's money I was spending——'

'What do you mean?' she asked him sharply. 'Papa, you aren't starting up in business again?'

'Of course not. Relax!' her father told her. 'Oh well, the secret's out. I said to Leon how it would be when you got to know about it.'

'About what? Are you working on something together?' Nita was bewildered.

'After a manner of speaking. Leon's always wanted me to stay on in an advisory capacity when he took over. He said he'd like to be able to call upon my experience from time to time. I told him the last thing that he wanted was his predecessor poking his nose in, but he insisted—made it a condition of the contract. It's a non-executive role, of course, but it'll stop me going completely to seed.' Her father's tone was offhand, but he sounded pleased nevertheless. 'I knew you would only start worrying as to whether I'd be able to handle it, so I kept quiet about it all and told Leon to do the same.'

'Did you indeed?'

'I was going to tell you eventually. I suppose it would have come out in the end. I didn't like deceiving you.' Diego's tone was faintly wheedling. 'I'm not going to overdo it, Nita, I promise you that, but I have to do something. Can you see me watching television all day long? I'd be dead from boredom inside six months!'

'I suppose so,' she allowed.

'Then I've got your blessing?' he asked.

'If it'll make you happy. Not that I don't know that you'd go ahead regardless of anything I said about it.'

'Maybe,' her father conceded. 'But I wouldn't enjoy it, believe me.'

'And you'll take care?'

'Of course. I want to live to see my grandchildren, don't I?'

He'd better plan on living for a good few years yet, in that case, Nita decided as she put the phone down at last. The way she was feeling at the moment about love and marriage, it looked like being an age before she contemplated anything of the kind. If ever.

She frowned. So Leon had insisted on engaging her father's services. She wondered why. If it had been anyone else, the reason might have been obvious. But not with Leon.

'Problems at home? Your father is all right, isn't he?' Maria asked, noticing her preoccupation.

'Yes, he's fine, thanks.'

'So? What are you looking so worried about?'

'He's just told me he's working again.' Nita explained the situation as briefly as she could.

'You're worried that he'll overdo it?'

'No. I think he's got enough sense now not to do that.'

'Then what's the matter?' asked Maria.

'I was wondering why Leon had done it. There must be any number of people he could call upon to advise him—younger, fitter people than my father. If he needs advice, that is. Personally, I'd have thought he was the last person in the world to depend on other people's opinions.'

'You're probably right there.'

'Then why has he done it?' Nita sighed.

'I imagine he was being kind. He knew what it would do to your father to let go completely, so he's given him a chance to keep his hand in. It's the sort of thing that Leon would do.'

'Kindness is the last quality that I'd attribute to him,' Nita said with a snort of disbelief. 'He's utterly ruthless!'

'Is he? Perhaps you don't know him as well as you think you do.'

'Don't I?'

'I don't know what went wrong between you, Nita, and I'm not going to pry, so don't worry.' There was a note of censure in Maria's voice. 'But don't ever try and tell me that Leon Calveto isn't one of the most generous men around. Five years ago, when Emilio was going through a very bad patch with the business, Leon gave us all the help he could.'

'He's a rich man. He can afford it.'

'Not just money,' Maria said quietly. 'Although he lent us as much as we needed and offered more, with no immediate prospect of getting it back. But, more important, he gave us his time and made every effort to put business our way. Things picked up, thank God, and we were able to get back on our feet again. We paid back the money. But we'll always owe him for the support he gave us when we needed it.'

'Emilio's a friend of his,' Nita reminded her. 'I expect he was glad to help——'

'As glad as he was to help quite a few other people who've been in similar situations, who weren't friends of his. Leon himself would be the first to tell you that he's no plaster saint. He's got his faults—we all have. But he's not as black as you're painting him.'

'I'm sorry,' Nita said stiffly. 'I shouldn't have——'

'I'm sorry too.' Maria looked contrite. 'I didn't mean to lecture you. My tongue runs away with me sometimes.'

'It's all right, I understand.'

'Do you?' Maria hesitated, then put her hand on Nita's and squeezed it sympathetically. 'I'm sorry, I shouldn't have spoken to you like that. But I meant every word of it. Think about it, will you? Maybe you got a few wires crossed somewhere along the line.'

'Maybe.' Nita preferred to drop the subject. 'Tell me, did you buy that filigree necklace that you were raving about? The one that you saw at the little silversmith's shop near the market?'

Maria accepted the lead she was given. Perhaps she thought she had said enough for the moment. 'I'm still dithering. Tomorrow you must come with me and have a look at it, then you can tell me what you think.'

And so the rest of the evening passed with both girls carefully avoiding any further discussions of a serious nature. Emilio came home from the office with tales of woe about a difficult party of tourists which had them in gales of unsympathetic laughter, and dinner, which might have been an awkward affair if Maria had chosen to pursue the subject of Leon, was a relaxed, fairly hilarious occasion.

But, later, as Nita prepared for bed, she found herself going over the conversation again. Was Maria right? Had she misjudged Leon? Mercedes had certainly told her a likely tale and one which she had rushed headlong to believe. But what if it wasn't true? Nita's mind reeled as she tried to grapple with the matter once again. Of course Mercedes wasn't an entirely disinterested party. Could she have lied?

And if she had lied, what did it mean? That Leon had been genuinely interested in her, not merely as a tool to help him to a successful take-over, but as a person in her own right? Or did it? If he cared, he would have told her by now. Wasn't it more likely that he saw her just as an attractive body that he wouldn't mind possessing? She had said that to him when she had confronted him in his office and he hadn't denied it. He had just told her to go.

Could she have been mistaken? After all, he had tried to talk to her later and she hadn't been prepared to listen to him. She argued round and round the subject until she didn't know what to believe any more.

A photograph in the gossip column of one of the next day's papers went a long way to resolving her doubts. 'Calveto dances the night away,' the headline ran, and the accompanying piece went on to identify his escort at the nightclub as Mercedes—an unnecessary piece of information. Nita had already recognised the small figure clinging adoringly to him, her face alight with the glow of possession.

So much for the possibility, however remote, that he might just have cared! Nita laughed. She must stop clutching at straws and face reality. Leon only spelled disaster, and the sooner she stopped tormenting herself, the better it would be for her.

She threw herself enthusiastically into the social life available to her. Maria and Emilio were a popular couple, involved in almost every aspect of the town's affairs, and the invitations that flowed in for them made a point of including their visitor. Most of their friends were youngish married couples like themselves, but Nita had no lack of escorts at the gatherings that she attended with them. The news that they had a young, attractive female staying with them had circulated to every unattached male in town—or so it seemed.

Up until now she hadn't really been interested. None of the men she had met had come near Leon in attractiveness. His image had come between her and every man who had talked to her.

Well, it wasn't going to happen any more. Nita forced herself to be good company, to laugh and flirt and generally project an image of a girl who was enjoying herself. She made herself listen when people talked to her about themselves. She accepted offers to dance where before she had given a polite refusal.

'You're making quite a hit,' Maria told her after one evening, a fund-raising dinner-dance, held for charity, when Nita had attracted a good deal of attention from the opposite sex. 'I don't think you had the same partner twice, did you? They were queueing up for you!'

There was safety in numbers, Nita thought, her mind going back inevitably to another evening, not long before, when she had danced all night with the same partner: Leon. When she had been aware of nothing but the movement of his body against her, the slight roughness of his cheek as he pressed it to hers, the firmness of his arms holding her. Was she never going to forget?

Maria was talking excitedly to her husband about some project that she had in mind, and Nita surfaced rapidly when the other girl turned to her and asked her opinion. 'It would be a good idea, wouldn't it, Nita? You would enjoy it?'

She started. 'Sorry, I didn't quite catch what you were saying——'

'I was telling Emilio what a lovely thing it would be for us to hold a party while you're here with us. I do love entertaining, and it would be such fun to do something like that before I get all fat and ungainly and only want to hide away and not talk to people.'

Emilio gave a bellow of laughter. 'I doubt that day will ever come!'

'Beast!' Maria gave him an indignant look and then returned to her theme. 'We could have fairy lights in the garden. And dancing. And I can get someone in to help with the food—and Rosa's got a sister who could help to serve it. Then there'd be the music. Who were those people who played at the Rozos' a couple of months ago?'

'Los Castellanos, they called themselves. I know the guitarist, he works in one of the hotels between engagements. I expect he'd be glad of the job.'

'So you think it's a good idea?' Maria turned a delighted face towards him. 'Oh, Emilio, you're wonderful!'

'You look like a little girl who's just been given a present,' he chuckled.

'I feel like one. Oh, I'm going to enjoy myself!'

'And not overdo it, hm?' he cautioned.

'I'll see to that,' Nita volunteered. 'I'll do the running around and Maria can give the orders.'

'It sounds like a perfect division of labour to me,' said Maria. 'I'll warn you, though, that you'll be worn out by the time we've got it all set up.'

'I'm stronger than I look.'

'You'll need to be!' Emilio warned her. 'You don't know my wife when she gets the bit between her teeth. She's like someone possessed!'

Nita realised what he meant when the invitations went out the very next day to just about everybody that Maria knew. She had selected a date early in the following week.

'Not much notice, I know. But I don't think there's anything else going on that night. We'd have been invited to it if there was,' Maria said with the confidence of one who attends every social event of note. 'Anyway, the best parties are those that just happen.'

But she didn't intend leaving anything to chance. Every last detail, from the hanging of the fairy lights in the garden to the choice of fillings for the savoury pasties that were part of the menu, passed under her eagle eye.

'Not that I don't trust people, you know,' she told Nita, who was frantically urging her to rest. 'It's just that I always feel happier if I've supervised everything myself. I worry less about things going wrong.'

'And what could possibly go wrong? You've anticipated every disaster.'

'Well, there's always the weather. I haven't thought about what we'll do if there's an absolute downpour and no one wants to venture out that night.'

'Miss one of your parties? Never!' Emilio told her. 'So stop worrying.'

By the day of the party Nita was worn out with all the dashing over town in search of this and that which Maria was sure would add to the occasion. But a siesta in the afternoon did a lot to rest her, and, as she dressed for the evening ahead, she found that she was almost looking forward to it.

Maria had bullied her into buying one of the local *huipiles*, a long, loose shift made of white silky

material, trimmed round the neck and hem with
brilliant embroidery. Nita liked herself in it. The
simple style suited her, she knew, emphasising the
slender curves of her figure and the tawny glow that
the sun had given her complexion during her stay
here. She left her hair loose against her shoulders,
merely clipping it away from her face with jewelled
combs that she had found at the same time that she
had bought the dress.

'You'll break a few hearts tonight,' Emilio said
admiringly as she emerged from her room and joined
them to receive their guests. 'Won't she, Maria?'

'Just as long as yours isn't one of them!' Maria
tapped his arm in pretended jealousy. Then she smiled
at Nita. 'You do look lovely. I hope you enjoy yourself
tonight. You deserve to after all the hard work that
you've put in.'

'And so do you.'

'That's enough of the mutual admiration. I just heard
the doorbell, I think the first guests are arriving,'
Emilio told them, and that was the end of private
conversation between them for quite some time as they
devoted themselves to receiving partygoers.

Nita knew most of the people who came, by sight, if
not always by name. When the band started to play she
took to the floor with one of Emilio's brothers and then
danced with a youth she had met at a dinner party two
nights before. Then a cousin of Maria's, called Julio
Perez, claimed her.

'You're the most gorgeous girl in the room,' he said
conversationally as he whirled her round, expertly
avoiding the other dancers, with his attention apparently
all upon her. 'And not just the room—the most
gorgeous girl in Merida. You're not going to dance with

anyone else for the rest of the evening. You're mine, all mine.'

He was only a year or two older than herself, an agricultural economist working on a project to educate farmers about the best use of their land and new farming methods. He was back in Merida for a holiday, but he was based at a research institute in Mexico City.

'My home,' she told him, and he laughed delightedly.

'Fate, that's what it is! I'll see you when I get back there. I'll take you out dancing. It's a date, yes?'

'It's a date, maybe,' she said, laughing.

'Spoilsport! Still, I have got all evening to convince you that I'm the nicest man you ever met. You never know, I might just manage it.'

He was fun, was Julio—lively, uncomplicated and clearly smitten with her.

'Tell me,' he said when, after a pause for a rest and a cool drink, they danced again, 'is there some special boy-friend in your life?'

'No, no one special,' Nita admitted. She wasn't going to think about Leon tonight.

'I can't think why not,' he said with frank admiration. 'The guys in Mexico City must be even slower than I thought they were.'

Nita only laughed. He was outrageous, she thought. But he was fun. She wasn't going to take him seriously—no danger of that. But it looked as if the evening was going to be more enjoyable than she had thought it would be. They ate supper together and danced some more, this time to slower, dreamier music.

Julio was nice, she was thinking. Nice enough to make her forget Leon? She didn't know. But certainly nice.

When suddenly his voice broke in on her thoughts. 'You did say there wasn't anyone special in your life at the moment, didn't you?'

'Yes. Why?' She looked at him in surprise.

'Because there's a guy standing over there against a wall who looks as if he'd like to break every bone in my body. And, as I don't know him from Adam, I just wondered why.'

Nita turned quickly within the circle of his arms to look, and the room spun giddily around her. What was Leon doing here?

'Do you know him?' asked Julio.

'We've met,' she said through dry lips. 'He doesn't matter. Let's dance.'

'You've gone a bit pale. Are you all right?'

'Yes—no.' She had to get away from Leon. 'Perhaps a little air——'

'Of course.' He sounded worried about her. 'I'll take you outside.'

In the warm humidity of the garden there wasn't much air, but at least she was away from Leon in a little sheltered grove a distance from the house. Only then he was there, looming suddenly up at them.

'Take your hands off her, do you hear?'

Julio took his supporting arm away from her, but only to square up to the newcomer. 'I don't like your tone.'

'And I don't like anything about you!' There was a suppressed fury in Leon's voice that scared Nita. 'She belongs to me—do you understand? Now get out of my sight before I do you an injury!'

'The lady didn't tell me she had an escort for the evening.' Julio stood his ground.

'She didn't know I'd be here.'

Somehow Nita found her voice. 'Don't listen to him, Julio. He's not——'

Julio didn't appear to hear her. He was too intent on clearing himself with Leon. Why were Mexican men so punctilious in matters of male honour? Steal a man's car and he would forgive you—just. Steal a man's woman and he would get his revenge if it took him the rest of his life. Julio clearly didn't feel inclined to involve himself in a dispute of that kind.

Leon cut short his stumbling excuses and sent him indoors. He went without another glance at Nita.

'Your Romeo didn't have much spunk when it came down to it, did he?' Leon jeered, watching him go.

'He's not my Romeo!'

'Isn't he? From what I've seen he seemed to be doing pretty well.' He turned back to her. 'Or do you go into the garden with every man?'

'How dare you!' Her hand made stinging contact with his face. And then she made to run from him.

He caught her before she had taken two steps. 'You're not going anywhere, Nita. I have to talk to you.'

'I don't want to listen!'

'Damn you, Nita!' His voice was ragged. 'For heaven's sake——' He pulled her towards him with a force that she couldn't resist and his mouth came down on hers in a punishing kiss.

She'd missed him—oh, how she'd missed him! The touch of him against her, rousing her, stirring her to a wild abandon that she couldn't damp down. It didn't matter what he was or what he felt for her. Nothing mattered except the warmth of his body as he held her closer to him and the slow fire ran through her veins.

She could hardly bear it when he finally raised his lips from hers.

'Well,' he said slowly, his eyes scanning her face in

the dim light that came from the myriad coloured globes scattered throughout the greenery, 'so you don't belong to me. You've a strange way of showing it.' He kissed her again, gently this time, his mouth moving over her skin with tantalising softness. 'Tell me you want me, Nita. Let me hear you say it.'

'I want you.' It was only the truth.

Leon pulled her closer to him. 'And I've never stopped wanting you. Do you know that? From the first time I saw you I knew I had to have you.'

'But you despised me.'

'At first. Can you blame me? I thought you were a cold-blooded little bitch who didn't give a damn about anybody. You certainly did your best to give me that impression. But I still wanted you. I hated myself as much as I told myself I hated you, but you were a fever in my blood. I couldn't shake you off.' His lips sought hers again. 'When you accused me of making love to you just to get my hands safely on your father's business you couldn't have been farther from the mark. I was getting to the stage where nothing mattered a damn except making love to you. You were driving me wild!'

'Yet you didn't take me when you had the opportunity.'

He laughed harshly. 'I called myself all sorts of fool that night. But I was scared.'

'Scared?' queried Nita.

'That you'd change your mind in the morning. That you would despise me for taking advantage of you. That you'd despise yourself for giving in. That——' He shook his head dazedly. 'I couldn't believe my luck that night. But I didn't dare to take the chance in case it all ended there.' His arms hugged her closer to him. 'I didn't want a one-night stand. I knew that wouldn't satisfy me.'

'And next day——'

'Next day I cursed myself for holding back. It seemed as if I'd lost you anyway. You told me you hated me. You wouldn't listen when I tried to reason with you. I decided to leave it until after my deal with your father had gone through. I thought then you'd know that I hadn't any ulterior motive for seeking you out, but you wouldn't listen then either. I looked for you at the end of the signing session, but you'd vanished from sight. I was up to my eyes in work that week, meetings night and day. I told Mercedes to ring you and explain that I'd be in touch when I was free. She said that she tried several times, but you kept putting the phone down on her when she started to deliver the message. She said you told her you weren't interested.'

'She said that, did she?' Nita asked. Mercedes was going to have a little explaining to do some time in the near future!

'It seemed that you meant what you said,' Leon went on. 'You did despise me. You wouldn't even respond that day in Rivera's office when I kissed you. The only means of communication that we had, and even that seemed to be gone. I didn't know what to do.'

'So you let me go to Merida while you thought things out?'

'More or less. I told myself I was a fool to bother. I took other women out. Mercedes——'

'She told me once you always went back to her in the end,' Nita told him.

'A couple of times perhaps, between other affairs. She was a useful stopgap.' He saw the expression on her face. 'She was willing. She wanted me.'

But not just as a stopgap, Nita could bet. 'And I didn't want you.' If only he knew what she had been going through in the last few days!

'Your father told me you were having a wonderful time,' said Leon, 'And so did Maria.'

'You rang her?'

'Of course I rang her. I didn't know what to do. Nothing worked. I didn't want other women, I only wanted you. I asked her advice in the end. I was desperate. She suggested that a little civilised discussion between us might clear the air a little. She told me to come out here.'

'A civilised discussion? Is that what you call your behaviour tonight?'

He had the grace to smile. 'O.K.—I behaved badly.'

'That's one way of putting it!' said Nita darkly.

'When I arrived and saw you dancing with that boy, smiling up at him as if you cared something for him, I could have killed him with my bare hands! When he brought you out into the garden I was in such a blind rage I didn't know what I was doing. Heaven help me, I was so jealous!'

'Jealous? You?' echoed Nita.

'Is it so surprising?' he asked.

'Do I mean that much to you?'

'And more.'

'Well, now you've got me,' she told him. 'I'm yours for as long as you want. And afterwards——'

'What do you mean, "afterwards"?' His grip tightened on her. 'Nita, what on earth do you think I'm suggesting?'

'You're suggesting that we have an affair. Aren't you?'

'I'm suggesting we get married.'

'Married!' she gasped.

'Isn't that what people in love generally do?' Leon sounded slightly defensive.

'People who are in love, yes. But you——'

'I love you, Nita. I've never said that to a woman in my life before and I swear I won't say it to a woman again.'

'But you told me that men didn't marry girls from nightclubs. You said that——'

'I said a lot of things I didn't mean. I was terrified you'd fall for someone else. I was terrified of committing myself. I've never wanted anyone to marry me before. It's never gone that far.'

Nita gave a gurgle of laughter, joy springing up inside her. 'I can see that I'm going to be married to a complete neurotic!'

'Then you'll have me?'

'Try and stop me,' she smiled. 'I love you too. But there's one condition.' As he made to kiss her, she held him off.

'Anything you like.'

She smiled up at him. 'Top billing at all the nightclubs that you own?'

'So long as you don't seduce the customers,' he teased.

'Darling, I've——' She was about to tell him exactly how inexperienced she was. Then she stopped. Let him find that out for himself. 'Done,' she agreed.

Leon kissed her again, and for a long time there was silence.

Suddenly Nita raised her head as a thought struck her. 'I wonder what my father will say?'

She saw his lips twitch with amusement. 'Your father will congratulate himself on his business acumen at having driven a hard bargain with me for his business, when, as his future son-in-law, I might well have suggested receiving it as a wedding gift. After all, he did suggest that to me once before.'

'You mean?'

'I mean that I was the man that your father had in mind for you all along.'

'*You!*' she gasped.

'Yes, I was the man he wanted you to meet three years ago. I wish I'd met you then. It would have given me three years longer with you.'

'I might have disliked you on sight,' Nita pointed out.

'I'm sure you would have done.' His eyes danced mockingly. 'Three years ago I was insufferable.'

'And now?'

'And now I'm a reformed man.'

She laughed. 'Let's go in and tell Maria and Emilio.'

'Later,' he said his lips seeking hers.

And later, much later, they did.

## THE PEOPLE OF THE SUN

On her bedside table, Nita has a stylized picture of an Aztec warrior god—one of the many gods worshiped by the ancient Aztecs. The Aztecs inhabited central Mexico for hundreds of years before the arrival of the Spanish conquistadores in the sixteenth century. An advanced people, they built amazing cities of great temples and pyramids, beautiful palaces and even scientific observatories to study the stars. Unfortunately, their religion included a gruesome ritual—the sacrifice of living human beings to the sun god.

In Aztec mythology, before the world was created everything was darkness. The sun god refused to move across the sky until the other gods had fed him with their blood. The Aztecs, calling themselves "People of the Sun," believed it was their duty to make sure that the sun god was fed, to insure that the sun would travel across the sky every day.

The unfortunate victims sacrificed to the sun were often slaves or prisoners of war. At the same time it was considered an honor to be sacrificed, because the Aztecs believed that the soul of the victim went to heaven as one of the Quauhteca or Eagle People. And after four years of journeying with the sun, they came back to Earth as hummingbirds!

Although human sacrifice is barbaric, the Aztecs did leave behind many good things. For instance, their capital city, Tenochtitlán, became modern-day Mexico City. And the ruins of Aztec temples and palaces with their elaborate stone carvings are among the most beautiful and fascinating treasures that survive from the ancient world.

# Great old favorites...
# Harlequin Classic Library

The **HARLEQUIN CLASSIC LIBRARY**
is offering some of the best in romance fiction—
great old classics from our early publishing lists.

Complete and mail this coupon today!

## Harlequin Reader Service

In U.S.A. 1440 South Priest Drive
Tempe, AZ 85281

In Canada 649 Ontario Street
Stratford, Ontario N5A 6W2

Please send me the following novels from the Harlequin Classic Library. I am enclosing my check or money order for $1.50 for each novel ordered, plus 75¢ to cover postage and handling. If I order all nine titles at one time, I will receive a FREE book, *District Nurse*, by Lucy Agnes Hancock.

☐ 118 **Then Come Kiss Me**
   Mary Burchell

☐ 119 **Towards the Dawn**
   Jane Arbor

☐ 120 **Homeward the Heart**
   Elizabeth Hoy

☐ 121 **Mayenga Farm**
   Kathryn Blair

☐ 122 **Charity Child**
   Sara Seale

☐ 123 **Moon at the Full**
   Susan Barrie

☐ 124 **Hope for Tomorrow**
   Anne Weale

☐ 125 **Desert Doorway**
   Pamela Kent

☐ 126 **Whisper of Doubt**
   Andrea Blake

| | |
|---|---|
| Number of novels checked @ $1.50 each = | $ _____ |
| N.Y. and Ariz. residents add appropriate sales tax | $ _____ |
| Postage and handling | $ _____ .75 |
| TOTAL $ | _____ |

I enclose _____
(Please send check or money order. We cannot be responsible for cash sent through the mail.)

Prices subject to change without notice.

Name _____
               (Please Print)

Address _____
                              (Apt. no.)

City _____

State/Prov. _____ Zip/Postal Code _____

Offer expires February 29, 1984                    30856000000

*Just what the woman on the go needs!*

# BOOK MATE

**The perfect "mate" for all Harlequin paperbacks**
**Traveling • Vacationing • At Work • In Bed • Studying**
**• Cooking • Eating**

Pages turn WITHOUT opening the strap.

"CLICK"

SEE-THROUGH STRAP

Reinforced back stays flat.

Built in bookmark.

BOOK MARK

BACK COVER
HOLDING STRIP

Perfect size for all standard paperbacks, this wonderful invention makes reading a pure pleasure! Ingenious design holds paperback books OPEN and FLAT so even wind can't ruffle pages— leaves your hands free to do other things. Reinforced, wipe-clean vinyl-covered holder flexes to let you turn pages without undoing the strap...supports paperbacks so well, they have the strength of hardcovers!

10″ x 7¼″, opened.
Snaps closed for easy carrying, too.